image comics presents

ROBERT KIRKMAN
CREATOR, WRITER

CHARLIE ADLARD
PENCILER, INKER

CLIFF RATHBURN
GRAY TONES

RUS WOOTON
LETTERER

CHARLIE ADLARD
&
CLIFF RATHBURN
COVER

SINA GRACE
EDITOR

THE WALKING DEAD, VOL. 14: NO WAY OUT. First Printing. Published by Image Comics, Inc. Office of publication: 2134 Allston Way, 2nd Floor, Berkeley, California 94704.

PRINTED IN THE USA. For information regarding the CPSIA on this printed material call: 203-595-3636 and provide reference # EAST – 71959

ISBN: 978-1-60706-392-6

YOU SLEEP?
BARELY. A FEW MINUTES HERE AND THERE, IT FELT LIKE.

SAME HERE. FEELS GOOD, RIGHT... THE NOT SLEEPING? I MEAN, WE CAN BE HONEST WITH OURSELVES, CAN'T WE?
I'M GLAD I'M FEELING IT, Y'KNOW? AFTER EVERYTHING WE'VE BEEN THROUGH... I'M TERRIFIED OF THE TIME WHEN THIS FEELS NORMAL.
IT'S GOOD TO KNOW I CAN STILL BE SCARED.

NOT SO SCARED YOU COULDN'T SAVE MY LIFE.
THANK YOU FOR THAT.
I'M SURE WE'RE FAR FROM EVEN THERE. BUT IT WAS AN AWESOME SHOT, WASN'T IT?

I'M STILL AMAZED. HOW IS IT YOU FOUND THEIR SHOOTER--I MEAN, THAT'S SOME LUCK THERE, YOU SPOTTING THE GUY IN TIME TO, I MEAN...
...HE COULD HAVE KILLED ME.

HE WAS THE FIRST ONE I SAW, CLIMBING ON TOP OF THE AWNING AT THE BANK ACROSS FROM ME. I WAS ABOVE HIM.
HE'S THE REASON I NOTICED THE OTHERS AT THE GATE, POOR DUMB BASTARDS. WASN'T SURE HE WAS WITH THEM UNTIL HE PUT THE GUN ON YOU.
THAT'S WHY I DIDN'T POP HIM ON SIGHT...

CLOP! CLOP! CLOP!
WHAT IN--?!

CLOP! CLOP! CLOP! CLOP! CLOP!

IT'S AARON, HELP ME GET THE GATE OPEN!

OKAY-- CLOSE IT!

WHERE ARE YOU GOING?!

ERIC'S BEEN STABBED!

WHOA! WHOA!
WE'RE HERE, ERIC--WE'RE HERE. IT'S GOING TO BE OKAY.

OH, CALM DOWN-- IT'S NOT THAT BAD, CUT'S NOT DEEP. I'LL BE FINE.
GOT ME?
I GOT YOU-- COME DOWN.

LET ME HELP.

DOCTOR CLOYD-- OPEN UP!
WHAM! WHAM! WHAM! WHAM!

WHAT?!
OH, MY GOD-- BRING HIM INSIDE!
HEATH?
YOU LEAVE FOR A WEEK AND EVERYONE STARTS HOOKING UP...

WATER?
YEAH, THANKS.

THE WAITING-- IT'S THE WORST.
I CAN'T STOP THINKING ABOUT... LOSING HIM. I DON'T KNOW HOW MUCH BLOOD IT WAS, BUT IT SEEMED LIKE A LOT.
HE LOST A LOT.

AARON, WHAT HAPPENED OUT THERE?

THIS WOMAN WAS ALONE... COULDN'T SEE HER INTERACTING WITH OTHER PEOPLE, BUT WE WATCHED HER FOR TWO DAYS. SHE GATHERED FOR SUPPLIES, HUNTED...
...SEEMED NORMAL. SHE CRIED A LOT, I LOOK AT THAT AS A GOOD SIGN.
CONVERSATIONS WENT WELL, SHE SEEMED REAL NICE. WE WERE BRINGING HER BACK HERE.

THOUGHT WE'D MAKE IT LAST NIGHT, BUT IT WAS GETTING REALLY DARK AND WE CAME UP ON THIS HOUSE, SECURE, NICE--HAD SOME BEDS. SO WE STOPPED FOR THE NIGHT.
WE WOKE UP IN THE MIDDLE OF THE NIGHT TO HER STEALING ONE OF THE HORSES, ERIC WAS JUST TRYING TO TALK TO HER-- AND SHE--
SHE STABBED HIM.

I DIDN'T KNOW SHE WAS DANGEROUS... I HAD NO IDEA..
...HOW COULD I?

IT'S DONE.

ALL BETTER.
DOC PATCHED ME UP REAL GOOD.
OH, MY GOD--I WAS SO WORRIED. I CAN'T-- I--
COME HERE!

I TOLD YOU IT WASN'T THAT BAD. SHE JUST CUT ME--WASN'T EVEN THAT DEEP. LOST A LITTLE BLOOD-- BUT I'M FINE.
STILL HURTS REALLY BAD, THOUGH. THE HUG WAS A BIT MUCH.
SORRY, I--OH, GOD-- I'M JUST GLAD YOU'RE OKAY.

SO, YOU AND DENISE, HUH?
YEAH. I REALLY LIKE HER. I SPENT A LOT OF TIME WITH HER WHEN SCOTT WAS...IT JUST KIND OF HAPPENED.
ERIC'S FINE.

YEAH, DENISE TOLD US BEFORE SHE WENT TO CLEAN UP.
SPEAKING OF WHICH, I SHOULD PROBABLY HELP HER.

SO... NEVER A DULL MOMENT, HUH?
NO KIDDING, RIGHT? I MEAN... CHRIST.
I MISS THE DAYS... UGH... FEELS LIKE IT'S ALWAYS BEEN LIKE THIS.

SPEAKING OF WHICH, I SHOULD PROBABLY BE GETTING TO THE TOWER.
TOBIN'S PROBABLY WAITING TO DRIVE ME.

YOU OKAY TO GO OUT THERE? I MEAN, AFTER YESTERDAY, I FIGURED YOU MIGHT WANT TO TAKE SOME TIME OFF.

NOW THAT WE KNOW WHAT'S OUT THERE-- ISN'T IT MORE IMPORTANT I KEEP WATCH?
WE'RE ALL PULLING OUR WEIGHT, RICK. I'M HAPPY TO DO MY PART.
DON'T SWEAT IT, REALLY... I'M THE SAFEST ONE HERE WHEN I'M UP THERE.

KNOCK. KNOCK.

MORGAN? WHAT ARE YOU DOING HERE?
WHAT DO YOU WANT?

MY WIFE... SHE'S BEEN DEAD FOR A YEAR.
A YEAR.
I HOPE YOU CAN UNDERSTAND HOW I FEEL ABOUT THAT. I LOVED HER VERY MUCH AND... AND IT'S TAKEN A LONG TIME FOR ME TO GET USED TO THE IDEA THAT SHE'S DEAD.

I COMPLETELY UNDERSTAND THAT.
IT'S LIKE YOU SAID, WHAT WE DID WAS A MISTAKE.

I KNOW... AND IT WAS, FOR A LOT OF DIFFERENT REASONS...
BUT MICHONNE... I REALLY LIKE YOU. I DON'T KNOW IF I'M READY FOR WHAT WE DID... NOT YET.
BUT I REALLY WOULD LIKE TO GET TO KNOW YOU BETTER.

OKAY.
I WAS GETTING READY TO MAKE BREAKFAST. YOU WANT TO COME IN?
I'D LIKE THAT.

MORNING, SON. WHEN'D YOU GET UP?
I GOT UP WHEN YOU LEFT. I HEARD YOU CLOSING THE DOOR... WHERE'D YOU GO?

DIDN'T SLEEP WELL LAST NIGHT, WENT TO CHECK THE GATE, SEE HOW THINGS WERE ON THE OTHER SIDE OF THE FENCE.
YOU OKAY?

YEAH. WHY?
WHY? WE WERE ATTACKED YESTERDAY, I THOUGHT YOU MIGHT BE SCARED.

WELL, I'M NOT.
WHAT HAPPENED WAS A GOOD THING. NOW MAYBE EVERYONE WILL STOP PRETENDING WE'RE ALL SAFE.

CARL, I--

YEAH, DAD?

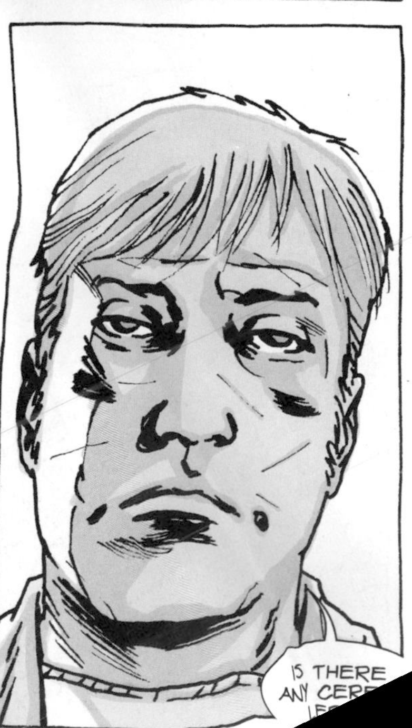
IS THERE ANY

OH, CRAP.

WRAMM!

DAMN!
DAMN!

HANG BACK, TOBIN!
I GOT THIS ONE!

SHUCK!

TOBIN-- GET INSIDE!
THERE'S MORE OF THEM COMING!

IT'S SO STIFF AND DIRTY.
WELL, IT'S HORSE HAIR, SOPHIA. THEY DON'T USE A LOT OF CONDITIONER. NOT AS MUCH AS YOU OR I AT LEAST.
YOU STILL WANT ME TO TEACH YOU HOW TO RIDE HER?
HEY, MAGGIE...

YOU GOT EVERY RIGHT TO YELL AT ME.
I'M SO DAMN SORRY ABOUT THAT HORSE. I KNOW YOU TRUSTED US WITH IT... AND WE LOST IT. I WISH I COULD MAKE IT UP TO YOU.

AARON, PLEASE. I KNOW WHAT HAPPENED.
HOW'S ERIC?

HE'S GOING TO BE FINE. I MIGHT HAVE OVERREACTED A LITTLE--I GUESS THE WOUND WASN'T SO BAD--BUT WHAT THE HELL, I'M NO DOCTOR. I SEE BLOOD, I FREAK.
YOU REALLY NOT MAD ABOUT THE HORSE?

NO, I'M REALLY NOT. I KNOW YOU TRIED EVERYTHING YOU COULD TO KEEP THAT WOMAN FROM STEALING HER--BUT THE TRUTH IS I'M KIND OF GLAD SHE'S GONE.
THIS PLACE IS GOOD FOR US--BUT NOT FOR THEM. THAT'S WHY I OFFERED FOR YOU AND ERIC TO TAKE THEM OUT IN THE FIRST PLACE.
WE DON'T HAVE ROOM IN HERE--I CAN'T KEEP THEM IN A BACKYARD FOR WEEKS ON END. THEY NEED WIDE OPEN SPACES.
I JUST HOPE THAT WOMAN, WHOEVER SHE IS, TAKES CARE OF BUTTONS. I HOPE SHE'S HAPPY.

THANKS, I JUST WANTED TO COME BY AND CHECK IN ON YOU, MAKE SURE YOU'RE GETTING BY OKAY.
I BROUGHT SOME FOOD.
NO, NO-- THANK YOU. PLEASE, COME IN. HAVE A SEAT. THANK YOU SO MUCH FOR BRINGING THIS.

IS RON AROUND? I WAS GOING TO BRING CARL WITH ME, BUT HE'S GOT HIS NOSE STUCK IN SOME BOOK HE SEEMS TO LOVE. SO HE WANTED TO STAY AND READ.

HE'S STILL IN HIS ROOM, DON'T THINK HE WOULD HAVE BEEN GOOD COMPANY FOR CARL ANYWAY.
SO IT'S FOR THE BEST.

SO, HOW IS HE DOING NOW? THINGS OKAY?
WE'RE FINE. WE'RE GETTING BY. IT'S HARD, AS I'M SURE YOU KNOW.
SOMETIMES YOU JUST DON'T KNOW WHAT TO SAY TO THEM, YOUR KIDS... Y'KNOW?

WHAT YOU SAID AT THE FUNERAL, THAT'S HELPED... THAT'S REALLY HELPED A LOT WITH WHAT TO SAY TO HIM.

I'VE BEEN MEANING TO THANK YOU FOR THAT. IT'S BEEN A BIG HELP. AND IT WAS...
...VERY KIND.

IT WAS THE TRUTH AS I SEE IT. NOTHING MORE.
I WAS HAPPY TO SPEAK ON YOUR HUSBAND'S BEHALF, WHAT HAPPENED... I'M NOT GOING TO SAY IT WASN'T HIS FAULT, BUT... IT'S NOT FAIR TO BLAME IT ALL ON HIM.

DOUGLAS?
THE DOOR WAS UNLOCKED, I WAS TOLD YOU WERE IN HERE.

HELLO?

DOUGLAS, PEOPLE ARE **WORRIED** ABOUT YOU...

DOUGLAS?
DAMN IT... IT'S STARTING TO **SNOW**.

AS YOU CAN SEE BEHIND ME, OUR RECENT GUNPLAY HAS DRAWN QUITE A BIT OF ATTENTION OUR WAY.
WE'VE GOT TWICE AS MANY ROAMERS SURROUNDING THIS PLACE AS WE USUALLY DO--AND THEY ALL SHOWED UP TODAY. SO WE'RE GOING TO CLEAN THEM OFF.
SINCE GUNS ARE WHAT DREW THEM HERE--WE AIN'T USING THEM. HACK INTO THEIR HEADS, BASH THEIR SKULLS IN--WHATEVER YOU HAVE TO DO, BUT DO IT *QUIETLY*.

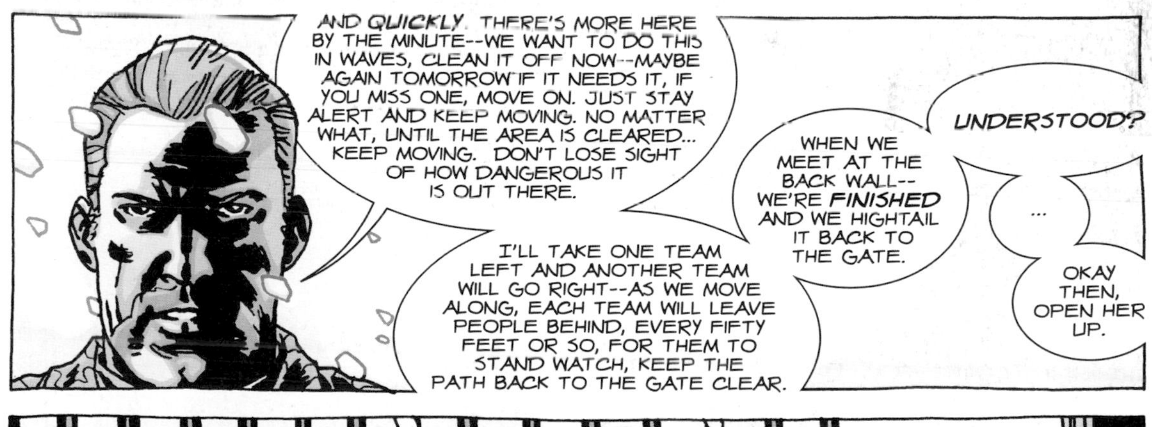
AND *QUICKLY*. THERE'S MORE HERE BY THE MINUTE--WE WANT TO DO THIS IN WAVES, CLEAN IT OFF NOW--MAYBE AGAIN TOMORROW IF IT NEEDS IT, IF YOU MISS ONE, MOVE ON. JUST STAY ALERT AND KEEP MOVING. NO MATTER WHAT, UNTIL THE AREA IS CLEARED... KEEP MOVING. DON'T LOSE SIGHT OF HOW DANGEROUS IT IS OUT THERE.
I'LL TAKE ONE TEAM LEFT AND ANOTHER TEAM WILL GO RIGHT--AS WE MOVE ALONG, EACH TEAM WILL LEAVE PEOPLE BEHIND, EVERY FIFTY FEET OR SO, FOR THEM TO STAND WATCH, KEEP THE PATH BACK TO THE GATE CLEAR.
WHEN WE MEET AT THE BACK WALL--WE'RE *FINISHED* AND WE HIGHTAIL IT BACK TO THE GATE.
UNDERSTOOD?
...
OKAY THEN, OPEN HER UP.

HERE WE GO!

LET'S MOVE!
KRAKK!

DID YOU PUT RICK IN CHARGE?
WHAT DOES IT MATTER?
WHAT DO YOU MEAN, "WHAT DOES IT MATTER?!"

REGINA HAS DIED, AARON. THE COMMUNITY IS A SHAM.
WE'RE NOT SAFE HERE. WE NEVER WERE-- NOT MORE THAN WE ARE OUTSIDE THESE WALLS.
SO WHY DOES IT MATTER WHO LEADS--WHO'S "IN CHARGE?"
MAYBE WITH RICK, WE STAND A CHANCE.

DAMN IT-- THERE'S MORE THAN WE THOUGHT!

THWACK!

SPENCER, YOU STAY HERE. BACK TO THE WALL, KEEP AN EYE OUT.
GLENN, LOOK...

OH, CRAP.

MAYBE YOU'RE RIGHT ABOUT RICK. HIS CREW--THEY'VE GONE THROUGH A LOT. I HEARD ABOUT ANDREA TAKING THOSE GUYS OUT FROM THE BELL TOWER--AND THE BIG ONE--ABRAHAM, ISN'T IT? HE TOOK OVER FOR TOBIN AS LEADER OF THE CONSTRUCTION CREW...
...I DON'T KNOW, DOUGLAS. MAYBE THEY DO KNOW BETTER THAN US. JUST TOOK ME BY SURPRISE, YOU GIVING UP THE TOP SPOT.
BUT DON'T SAY THIS COMMUNITY IS A SHAM. YOU SHOULD TRY LEAVING FOR A WHILE AND COMING BACK HERE.

THIS PLACE IS A SHINING BEACON OF HOPE IN THE MIDDLE OF A WASTE LAND. I DO AGREE THAT IT'S NOT WITHOUT ITS FLAWS...
...BUT IT'S NOT TIME TO GIVE UP.

IN FACT, I CAME HERE TO TELL YOU THAT I'M NEVER LEAVING AGAIN.
WHAT?

WRAKK!
WE'VE GOT TO TIME THIS SO WE GET TO THE BACK WALL THE SAME TIME AS THE OTHER GROUP! I DON'T KNOW HOW MANY ARE BACK THERE AND I DON'T WANT THEM UP AGAINST IT ALONE!
HOLLY, STAY HERE AND KEEP OUR PATH CLEAR! THE REST OF YOU--FOLLOW ME!

YOU AND I TALKED ABOUT A TIME WHEN THERE WOULD BE NO ONE LEFT TO RECRUIT. THAT TIME IS NOW.
WE LUCKED OUT WITH RICK'S GROUP--BUT HAVE YOU THOUGHT ABOUT THE ODDS OF FINDING A GROUP LIKE THAT AGAIN?
IT'S MORE LIKELY THAT WE'LL FIND SOMEONE CRAZY OR DANGEROUS OR BOTH. I DO THE BEST JOB I CAN, SCREENING PEOPLE--BUT WHAT IF I ACCIDENTLY LET A GROUP LIKE THE ONE THAT JUST ATTACKED US IN?

OR WHAT IF RICK HAD BEEN WAY WORSE--AND WANTED TO BE LEADER, BUT YOU WEREN'T WILLING TO GIVE IT UP?
I DON'T WANT ANOTHER DAVIDSON SITUATION.

WE'RE ALMOST TO THE BACK WALL--KEEP MOVING!
KRAGG!

SHUKK!
UGH...
DIDN'T EXPECT THIS MANY.

BUT WHAT ABOUT OUR COMMUNITY? WE NEED MORE PEOPLE TO HELP US RUN IT--HELP US EXPAND.
ERIC WAS STABBED, ONE OF THE HORSES WAS STOLEN. I'M NOT GOING BACK OUT THERE. IT'S TOO DANGEROUS.
AND-- EXPAND?! WHAT'S THE POINT?! WE HAVE ENOUGH SPACE, ENOUGH PEOPLE TO KEEP THIS PLACE GOING, MORE THAN ENOUGH HOUSES BEHIND THE WALLS FOR PEOPLE TO LIVE IN.
WE NEED TO CHANGE THE WAY WE DO THINGS... START BEING MORE CAREFUL.

DOUGLAS, WHAT'S WRONG WITH YOU?

I JUST LOST MY WIFE, GOD DAMN IT!

ANOTHER CORNER... YOU GUYS READY?

GRUH.

YOU CALLING THE LAST ONE, ABRAHAM?

CALLED.
KRAK!

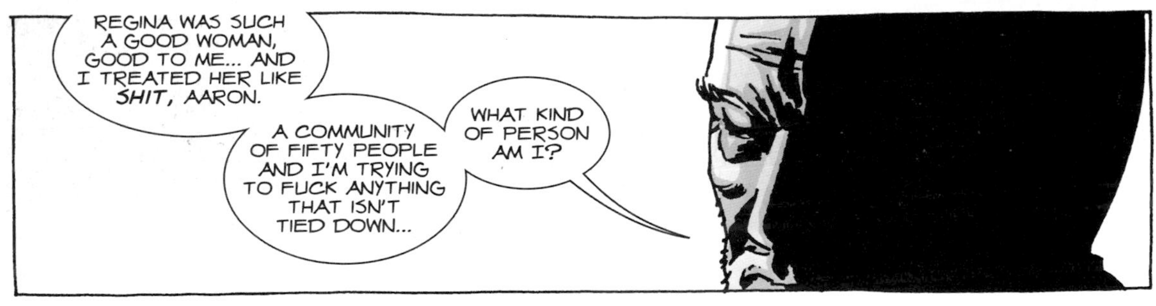
REGINA WAS SUCH A GOOD WOMAN, GOOD TO ME... AND I TREATED HER LIKE *SHIT*, AARON.
A COMMUNITY OF FIFTY PEOPLE AND I'M TRYING TO FUCK ANYTHING THAT ISN'T TIED DOWN...
WHAT KIND OF PERSON AM I?

OKAY, SO THAT WASN'T SO BAD.
WE'LL GIVE IT A DAY OR TWO AND THEN WE'LL PROBABLY HAVE TO DO THIS AGAIN. IT'S NOT GOING TO BE AN EASY WEEK OR SO COMING UP... BUT AS LONG AS WE STAY ON TOP OF IT, SHOULD BE MANAGEABLE.
THIS IS GODDAMN NERVE-WRACKING IS WHAT IT IS.
I CAN'T STAND THIS. IT'S MUCH BETTER WHEN YOU CAN JUST *AVOID* THEM. I *HATE* KILLING THEM.

THE TWO OF YOU LOVED EACH OTHER. I KNEW THAT, I THINK EVERYONE KNEW THAT.
I GOT NO QUALMS WITH WHATEVER TWO PEOPLE DO INSIDE THEIR RELATIONSHIP. I ALWAYS FIGURED THE TWO OF YOU HAD AN UNDERSTANDING.
DOESN'T MEAN IT'S WRONG.

SHE NEVER LIKED IT... JUST PUT UP WITH IT. THAT MAKES HER A BETTER PERSON, AND ME WORSE... COME TO THINK OF IT.
MORE THAN ANYTHING ELSE THOUGH...

I'M JUST SCARED, AARON.
FOR THE FIRST TIME SINCE WE CAME HERE, I'M TERRIFIED... OF WHAT'S OUT THERE, OF WHAT'S COMING... OF WHAT'S NOT COMING.
IT NEVER OCCURRED TO ME HOW INSECURE WE REALLY ARE.

I'M SCARED OF DYING.

PKOW!
WAS THAT--?!
WARNING SHOT! IT'S ANDREA!

SPLIT UP--WE MEET BACK AT THE GATE, GATHER YOUR PEOPLE-- MOVE!

WHAT WAS THAT?!
GUNSHOT OF SOME KIND.
CHRIST-- WHAT NOW?

MICHONNE-- WE'VE GOT TO GET TO THE GATE, FIND OUT WHAT'S GOING ON.
GET YOUR CHILD INSIDE, MA'AM!

THUNK!
WHAT'S GOING ON?!

DON'T KNOW. THERE'VE BEEN A FEW OF THEM COMING AT US SINCE WE STOPPED IN OUR POSITIONS--NOTHING WE CAN'T HANDLE.
I FIGURED SOMEONE ON THE OTHER SIDE GOT SWARMED AND HAD TO USE A GUN.

NO, IT'S WORSE THAT THAT.
THAT WAS A HIGH POWERED RIFLE. A WARNING SHOT FROM ANDREA.
C'MON!

WE'RE DONE HERE!
TO THE GATE.

FUCK ME.

IT'S A MOTHER-FUCKING HERD!
GET YOUR ASSES TO THE GATE BEFORE THEY BLOCK OUR WAY!

C'MON! HURRY!
GET THAT DAMN GATE OPEN!
WRAMM!

OH, SHIT!

THEY'RE ON TOP OF US!
GO ON!

BRUCE, HURRY UP!
GET IN HERE!

AARRGH!

DON'T CLOSE THF GATE!
BRUCE!

FUCKER!

GET THE CHAIN! WE GOTTA LOCK THIS DOWN!
GRAGH!

THUNK!

BRUCE... OH, MY GOD...

I DON'T WANT TO DIE!
OH, GOD--
HAKK!
I DON'T--

I--
GLK!

WHAT DO WE DO?

WRAKK!
WE DON'T HAVE TIME FOR THIS FUCKING SHIT.
OH, CHRIST...
OKAY... JUST... WE NEED TO SECURE THE GATE. CHAIN IT UP ON BOTH SIDES, USE WHATEVER EXTRA CHAIN WE HAVE--MAKE SURE IT'S SECURE.
AND THEN MOVE OUR MILITARY TRUCK IN FRONT OF IT... WE NEED TO BLOCK THEIR VIEW INSIDE, IF THEY SEE US, IT MIGHT WHIP THEM UP INTO A FRENZY AND WITH THAT MANY...
...I DON'T WANT TO THINK ABOUT WHAT COULD HAPPEN.

ABRAHAM, DON'T WALK AWAY...
I CAN'T BELIEVE YOU JUST--BRUCE WAS MY **FRIEND**, HE WAS--!

BRUCE WAS *DYING*. THERE WAS NOTHING WE COULD DO FOR HIM, HOLLY.

NOTHING YOU COULD DO? I'M GLAD YOU DIDN'T FEEL THAT WAY WHEN **TOBIN** LEFT ME TO DIE!
SMAKK!

BRUCE WAS BITTEN, HE WAS IN AGONY--I HAD TO PUT HIM OUT OF HIS MISERY. HE WAS MY FRIEND, TOO.
YOU THINK THIS IS EASY FOR **ME?**

OH, HONEY... I'M SORRY, I DIDN'T MEAN TO ATTACK YOU LIKE THAT, IT'S JUST... I'M SCARED.
THAT'S ALL. I'VE NEVER SEEN SO MANY OF THEM AT ONE TIME. HOW ARE WE EVER GOING TO GET THROUGH THIS?
WE'LL BE FINE, WE'LL FIGURE THINGS OUT.
DON'T TOUCH ME LIKE THAT.

SOMEONE MIGHT SEE US.

WHAT THE HELL ARE WE GOING TO DO?!
I MUST ASK YOU ALL TO REMAIN CALM. YOU'VE GOT EVERY RIGHT TO BE WORRIED, NICHOLAS, BUT I'VE CALLED THIS MEETING TO DISCUSS WHAT WE'RE GOING TO DO IN A CALM AND CIVIL WAY.
THERE'S NO NEED TO PANIC.
THE FIRST THING WE NEED TO DO IS KEEP AS QUIET AS POSSIBLE--STARTING NOW. WE'VE ALREADY SEEN THAT THE HERD IS MOVING AROUND THE PERIMETER OF THE FENCE--THEY'LL HAVE US SURROUNDED SOON... AND MORE ARE ARRIVING EVERY MINUTE, COMING FROM ALL DIRECTIONS.
LISTEN, THIS IS BAD, REALLY BAD. I'M NOT TRYING TO HIDE THAT, BUT I KNOW WE CAN GET THROUGH THIS, AND WE WILL. WE JUST NEED TO BE SMART ABOUT IT.
WHAT ABOUT FOOD? IF WE'RE TRAPPED HERE WE'RE NOT GOING TO BE ABLE TO GO OUT AND GATHER MORE.
WINTER IS HERE. WHAT DO WE DO IF WE RUN OUT?
WE'VE GOT ENOUGH FOOD TO LAST US AT LEAST A MONTH, AND IF WE START RATIONING NOW, LONGER THAN THAT. WE SHOULD BE OKAY.

GLENN IS RIGHT, JESSIE. FOR NOW, AT LEAST, FOOD IS NOT AN ISSUE.
MY MAIN CONCERN IS KEEPING THE WALLS UP. AS LONG AS THEY HOLD, WE'LL BE SAFE IN HERE AND WE'LL HAVE PLENTY OF TIME TO FIGURE OUT HOW WE'RE GOING TO GET RID OF ALL THE ROAMERS GATHERING AROUND US.
ABRAHAM, GATHER YOUR CREW AND SPLIT THEM INTO TEAMS. I'D LIKE THEM TO WALK THE PERIMETER OF THE FENCE AND SEARCH FOR ANY WEAK SPOTS.
IF THEY FIND ANY, WE NEED TO GET THOSE REINFORCED IMMEDIATELY. HAVE EVERYONE DO A COUPLE PASSES--I WANT TO MAKE SURE THERE'S NO CHANCE OF ANY OF THOSE PANELS COMING DOWN.
MICHONNE, I'D LIKE YOU TO ORGANIZE AND SCHEDULE A NIGHT-WATCHMAN PROGRAM. WE'RE GOING TO NEED TO HAVE A FEW PEOPLE KEEPING AN EYE ON THINGS AT ALL TIMES.
I DON'T WANT ANY SURPRISES WITH THIS MUCH DANGER ON OUR DOORSTEP. I WANT TO BE PREPARED FOR WHATEVER COMES.
TO THAT END, WE SHOULD PROBABLY STATION SOME PEOPLE ON THE ROOFS AT EACH CORNER OF OUR FENCE LINE--SO WE CAN KEEP AN EYE ON THE ROAMER ACTIVITY ON THE OTHER SIDE OF THE WALL.
WITH WINTER COMING, OUR SOLAR GRID IS GOING TO BE STRETCHED TO THE LIMIT AS IT IS TRYING TO KEEP US WARM. I'D RATHER NOT HAVE EVERYONE SPREAD OUT ANYWAY--SO I THINK WE'RE GOING TO NEED TO START SHARING HOUSES AGAIN.
I THINK IT'LL BE THE SAFEST THING, MOVING FORWARD.
I'M ALSO OPENING UP THE ARMORY. I WANT EVERYONE TO BE ABLE TO PROTECT THEMSELVES IN A WORST CASE SCENARIO SITUATION. SO STOCK UP, GRAB WHAT YOU'RE COMFORTABLE WITH.
THIS ISN'T MANDATORY, IF YOU'RE NOT COMFORTABLE WITH A GUN, PLEASE DON'T TAKE ONE. WE DON'T NEED AN ACCIDENT--AND WE DON'T NEED TO DRAW MORE OF THOSE THINGS TO US WITH ACCIDENTAL GUNFIRE.
WE'RE GOING TO BE WORKING OUT HOW BEST TO GET THESE THINGS AWAY FROM US--ALL I ASK IS YOUR CONTINUED CAUTION AND CALM AS WE DEAL WITH THIS SITUATION.
EVERYONE, THANK YOU FOR YOUR TIME.

DID YOU GET A READ ON THE CROWD, DOUGLAS? I'M WORRIED THIS MIGHT BE TOO MUCH FOR THEM TO HANDLE. I DON'T WANT PEOPLE TO PANIC.
HEY, RICK...

C'MON, LET'S GIVE DOUGLAS HIS SPACE...
WHAT ARE WE GOING TO DO ABOUT ANDREA? SHE'S STUCK IN THAT BELL TOWER ALL ALONE. I'M WORRIED ABOUT HER.

RIGHT NOW, TRUTH IS, SHE VERY WELL MAY BE THE SAFEST AMONG US.
SHE'S NOT A PRIORITY FOR NOW.

C'MON, MOM!
SORRY, RON. I'M COMING.

WELL, MORGAN. YOU READY TO TAKE A SHIFT ON MY NIGHT WATCH CREW?
WHY NOT? YOU KNOW I DON'T SLEEP VERY MUCH ANYWAY.

YOU DON'T HAVE TO WORRY ABOUT THAT ONE. ANDREA IS ONE OF *THEM.* THOSE PEOPLE DEALT WITH ALL KINDS OF CRAP LIKE THIS BEFORE THEY CAME HERE.
SHE'LL BE *FINE.*
I KNOW... I KNOW...

TRAPPED INSIDE? SO WHAT--I WAS NEVER PLANNING ON LEAVING AGAIN ANYWAY.
I HEAR YOU.

ROSITA, YOU GO ON AHEAD. HOLLY AND I ARE GOING TO GO TO THE ARMORY, MEET EVERYONE THERE TO ARM UP--AND THEN WE'RE GOING TO DO THE WALL-CHECK RICK ASKED FOR.
I'LL BE HOME A LITTLE LATE TONIGHT, I'M SURE.
I UNDERSTAND. LOVE YOU.
YOU, TOO.

YOU HAVE FUN WITH SOPHIA?
I WAS HELPING PEOPLE GET WEAPONS OUT OF THE ARMORY.
I DON'T *LIKE* GOING THERE. WHY'D YOU HAVE TO SEND ME OFF WITH THEM? WHY COULDN'T I STAY WITH YOU?

YOU GOT YOU A NEW BELT?
YEAH, THEY HAD A LEFT-HANDED ONE HERE, SO I SNAGGED IT.
AND THAT'S NOT ALL...

IS THAT *MINE?*

IT IS. THEY WERE JUST KEEPING IT IN THE ARMORY. I GOT MY OLD GUN BACK, TOO.
COOL.

IT'S LATE, ALMOST BED TIME, CARL.
I'LL JUST WEAR IT FOR A MINUTE.

OKAY, BUT JUST A MINUTE. YOU REMEMBER OUR RULE, RIGHT? YOU ONLY TAKE IT OUT OF THE BELT WHEN YOU NEED TO SHOOT IT.
I SEE YOU HOLDING IT WITHOUT NEEDING TO AND I'LL TAKE IT AWAY.
I REMEMBER.

HEY, DAD...?
YEAH?

I'M SCARED... BUT YOU CAN'T TELL. CAN YOU?

NO.
I SURE CAN'T, SON.

YEAH... I'M GOING TO BE A GOOD LEADER SOME DAY.
JUST LIKE YOU.

C'MERE.

KNOCK. KNOCK

I'M SORRY, RICK. I DON'T MEAN TO INTRUDE, BUT YOU'D SAID SOMETHING ABOUT GROUPING TOGETHER IN FEWER HOUSES AND..
...WITH EVERYTHING GOING ON, WE JUST...
WOULD IT BE OKAY IF WE SLEPT HERE TONIGHT?

SURE.
YEAH.
COME ON IN.

I'M REALLY SORRY TO DO THIS. WE DON'T HAVE TO STAY IF YOU--
JESSIE, PLEASE. REALLY, IT'S NO PROBLEM AT ALL.

HEY.
HEY.

LET ME GET SOME ROOMS SET UP FOR YOU.
WON'T TAKE A MINUTE.

I FUCKED UP... I FUCKED IT ALL UP.
NOW WE'RE ALL GOING TO DIE.

I FUCKED UP...

I'M SO SORRY, REGINA.

SO SORRY...
DAD?

OKAY, WE'LL SEE HOW THAT WORKS.
I'M SURE THEY'LL GET UP ONCE OR TWICE... OR WELL, CARL PROBABLY WILL.
RON, TOO. IT'S A NEW PLACE, HE'S PROBABLY EXCITED, WE SHOULD KEEP AN EAR OUT.

NO DOUBT.
THE SITUATION OUTSIDE SURE ISN'T GOING TO HELP.

I HOPE WE'RE NOT TOO MUCH TROUBLE. I KNOW THIS IS... WE DON'T KNOW EACH OTHER THAT WELL, AND...
JESSIE, PLEASE. IT'S FINE, REALLY.

I'VE GOT A PATROL SHIFT COMING UP IN A FEW HOURS AND I WAS GOING TO HAVE TO TAKE CARL OVER TO GLENN AND MAGGIE'S HOUSE-- BUT NOW I CAN JUST LEAVE HIM HERE WITH YOU.
IF THAT'S OKAY...

ABSOLUTELY.
NO PROBLEM AT ALL.

OKAY THEN...
OKAY...

CARL?
YOU AWAKE?

WHAT DO YOU WANT?

YOUR DAD KILLED MY DAD...

SO? MY DAD'S KILLED A LOT OF PEOPLE...

...AND SO HAVE I.

WHY'S YOUR DAD GET TO BE **GOOD** BUT MY DADDY IS **BAD?**

I DON'T KNOW.
IT'S JUST HOW THINGS **ARE.**

YOU HEAR THAT?
SOUNDS LIKE ONE OF THEM WAS UP, PROBABLY JUST GETTING A DRINK OR SOMETHING.

RICK...
...
...WHY DO YOU DO IT?

DO WHAT?

HELP PEOPLE... YOU COULD HAVE JUST LEFT PETE AND I ALONE, BUT YOU STUCK YOUR NOSE IN...
...YOU DIDN'T HAVE TO, AND IT WASN'T EASY, BUT YOU DID IT ANYWAY.

YOU WERE IN TROUBLE, HE WAS HURTING YOU AND YOUR SON. I JUST DID WHAT WAS RIGHT.
IT DOESN'T EVER REALLY OCCUR TO ME THAT I HAVE ANOTHER OPTION, JESSIE.

BUT YOU DO. LOOK AROUND YOU, NOBODY BLAMES ANYONE FOR JUST LOOKING OUT FOR THEMSELVES, NOT WITH ALL THAT'S GOING ON.

BUT I'VE HEARD THE STORIES FROM YOUR PEOPLE... YOU ALWAYS PUT YOURSELF OUT THERE, TRYING TO HELP OTHERS.
I THINK IT'S AMAZING.

IT'S *NOT.*

EVERYTHING I'VE DONE, FOR THE GOOD OF MY GROUP... HAS ALWAYS MOSTLY BEEN DONE TO PROTECT MY FAMILY.
THAT'S WHAT'S IMPORTANT TO ME.
PETE WAS DANGEROUS, HE WAS HURTING YOU... BUT IF HE'S DOING THAT, WHERE DOES IT END? EVENTUALLY THAT GETS OUT TO OTHER PEOPLE... PUTS THEM IN DANGER.

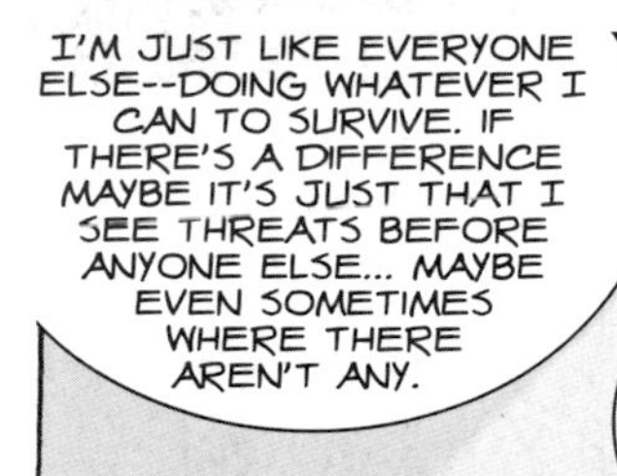

I'M JUST LIKE EVERYONE ELSE--DOING WHATEVER I CAN TO SURVIVE. IF THERE'S A DIFFERENCE MAYBE IT'S JUST THAT I SEE THREATS BEFORE ANYONE ELSE... MAYBE EVEN SOMETIMES WHERE THERE AREN'T ANY.
I DON'T KNOW...
SO I'M NO BETTER THAN THOSE WHO DIDN'T DO A THING.
BUT DON'T GET ME WRONG, AND I'M GLAD I HELPED YOU... BUT I WAS DOING IT TO KEEP MY SON SAFE.

YOU CAN ARGUE ALL YOU WANT, BUT I JUST DON'T SEE IT THAT WAY.
YOU'RE *SPECIAL.*

WELL, THANK YOU. REALLY.
I KIND OF... I SHOULD BE GETTING TO BED. I'VE GOT THAT PATROL COMING UP.

YEAH, SURE.
SORRY TO KEEP YOU UP.
GOOD NIGHT.

I'M SORRY, DID I WAKE YOU?
MORGAN HEY--NO, YOU DIDN'T. WHAT'S GOING ON?

I MISS MY WIFE AND I'M STILL NOT OVER HER DEATH AND I APPRECIATE YOU UNDERSTANDING ALL THAT.
BUT SOMETIMES I GET REALLY LONELY AND I JUST WANT TO BE WITH SOMEONE.
AND THAT DOESN'T MAKE ME A BAD PERSON.

IT DOESN'T AT ALL.
COME IN. WITH ALL THAT'S GOING ON, I DON'T THINK ANYONE WANTS TO BE ALONE.

GO AHEAD, I'LL MEET YOU IN THERE.

I HOPE YOU'RE NOT TOO COMFORTABLE UP THERE...

PLEASE, FATHER, I BEG YOU. WE HAVE GOOD PEOPLE HERE, I KNOW IT.
TAKE US UNDER YOUR WING AND DELIVER US FROM THE MOUTH OF EVIL THAT LAY AT OUR DOORSTEP...

JESUS.

WE'LL GET THROUGH THIS, IT'LL BE OKAY.
YOU'LL SEE.

ALL CLEAR?
ALL CLEAR.

...

RICK?
ARE YOU STILL AWAKE?

COULD I MAYBE... SLEEP NEXT TO YOU?
I'D FEEL SO MUCH SAFER.

JESSIE, I DON'T FEEL--

JESSIE.
PLEASE.

I CAN'T DO THIS...
I CAN'T.

RICK.

GLENN?

DID YOU GO ON PATROL?
WHY ARE YOU UP?
...

MY SHIFT DOESN'T START FOR ANOTHER HOUR. IT'S NOT THAT LATE, I JUST... I CAN'T SLEEP.

IT'S ANDREA. SHE'S UP IN THAT TOWER, ALL ALONE. SHE WASN'T PREPARED TO BE UP THERE... NOT OVERNIGHT.
AND RICK'S RIGHT... SHE'S *FINE* TONIGHT, BUT TOMORROW? THE DAY AFTER THAT? SHE'S GOING TO HAVE TO COME DOWN, FIND WATER, FOOD...

SHE'S GOING TO BE ALL ALONE, AND WE HAVE NO IDEA HOW LONG WE'RE GOING TO BE TRAPPED INSIDE LIKE THIS.
I CAN'T STOP THINKING ABOUT IT.

I'M SURE SHE'LL...
YOU'LL THINK OF SOMETHING TOMORROW. OKAY? YOU CAN GET SUPPLIES TO HER SOMEHOW.

YEAH.
GO BACK TO SLEEP, BABY. DON'T WORRY ABOUT ME.

I DON'T FEEL GUILTY.
I DON'T FEEL LIKE I DESERVE TO FEEL GUILTY. I'VE LIVED THROUGH HELL, MAYBE I'VE EARNED THIS.
I DESERVE TO BE HAPPY.

WHAT THE FUCK IS WRONG WITH YOU?
WHAT?

YOU ACT LIKE YOU'RE THE ONLY PERSON WHO'S LOST SOMEONE.
IT'S INSULTING.
I WASN'T MARRIED TO HIM... BUT I LOVED TYREESE. I LOVED HIM AND HE DIED. HIS FUCKING HEAD WAS CUT OFF WITH MY SWORD.

THAT'S HORRIBLE... AND YOUR SON DIED AND THAT'S ALSO HORRIBLE.
BUT THEY'RE DEAD AND WE'RE NOT. WE'RE ALIVE... SO WE LIVE.
CAN WE JUST GO BY THAT RULE?

AT A CERTAIN POINT YOU JUST HAVE TO MOVE ON.
I'M GOING TO GET A GLASS OF WATER.

I'M SORRY.
WHAT?
WHY?

YOU MUST THINK I'M A HORRIBLE PERSON. I KNOW WE SHOULDN'T HAVE DONE... WHAT WE DID.
PETE JUST DIED AND...
I BARELY EVEN KNOW YOU.
CHRIST. DO YOU THINK RON HEARD?

NO, JESSIE, REALLY... IT'S...
RON DIDN'T HEAR, THEY'RE BOTH ASLEEP... AND I DEFINITELY DO NOT THINK YOU'RE HORRIBLE.

OKAY... CALMING DOWN, NOW.
SORRY.

DON'T APOLOGIZE. REALLY.
IT'S OKAY. YOU'RE SURE YOU'RE GOING TO BE FINE HERE? I GOTTA START MY PATROL.
I'LL BE FINE HERE.
GO. I'LL SEE YOU SOON.

LORI...

YOU'RE NOT EVEN REAL.

RICK!
I WAS COMING TO GET--JUST FOLLOW ME!

WHAT IS IT?!

HOLY SHIT.
IT JUST HAPPENED-- WE DON'T KNOW HOW!
THE WALL'S BUILT ON I-BEAMS DRIVEN INTO THE GROUND. THEY HAMMER THOSE IN AND THEN BOLT THE PANELS TO THE BEAMS.

AT FIRST, I THINK HOLES WERE DUG AND CONCRETE WAS POURED INTO THE HOLES AROUND THE BEAMS TO KEEP THEM STURDY.
AT SOME POINT BEFORE WE GOT HERE... THEY RAN OUT OF CEMENT, JUST STARTED DIGGING HOLES AND PACKING DIRT AROUND THE BEAMS.
I'LL BE HONEST--IT SEEMED STURDY ENOUGH WHEN WE WERE DOING IT.

LOOK, WE MADE DUE WITH WHAT WE *HAD.*
THESE THINGS ARE BURIED FIVE FEET INTO THE GROUND-- THEY'RE STURDY AS HELL. THE HOLES DUG AROUND THEM ARE TIGHT--THE DIRT IS PACKED IN REALLY HARD.
THESE WALLS SHOULD HOLD.

THEY'RE NOT.

THIS ONE IS HOLDING... IT'S JUST... SAGGING. BUT THE DIRT IS HOLDING. IT'S NOT GOING ANYWHERE.
SEE?
WE COULD TRY TO PUSH BACK AGAINST THEM... BUT THAT WOULD JUST LOOSEN THE BEAM MORE.

OKAY, HERE'S WHAT WE'RE GOING TO DO. GET YOUR PICKUP TRUCK... WE'RE BACKING IT AGAINST THIS WALL. THAT WILL HELP SECURE IT, AT LEAST FOR NOW.
AND I WANT EVERY GODDAMN SECTION OF THIS WALL THAT ISN'T SECURED WITH CEMENT MARKED AND MONITORED UNTIL WE'RE THROUGH THIS.
THIS IS INSANE. IF THERE'S ANYTHING THAT CAN BE DONE TO FURTHER SECURE THESE PANELS *BEFORE* SOMETHING LIKE THIS HAPPENS... LET'S FIGURE THAT OUT.

OF COURSE, THE BEST THING WE COULD DO IS GET THE FUCKERS OFF THE WALL ONCE AND FOR ALL.
BUT I DON'T--

UH... I MIGHT ACTUALLY HAVE AN IDEA FOR THAT.

JUST BACK UP TO IT--SO THE TRUCK SUPPORTS IT. DON'T TRY TO PUSH IT CLOSED, THAT'LL JUST MAKE THE SUPPORT BEAM THAT MUCH WEAKER.
THAT'S IT.

WHAT DO YOU HAVE IN MIND?
ANDREA'S OUT THERE... SHE NEEDS SUPPLIES. SHE'S ALREADY GONE ONE NIGHT WITHOUT FOOD. I KNOW SHE ONLY BRINGS A LITTLE BIT WITH HER WHEN SHE GOES OUT.
HEATH AND I NEED TO GO OUT AND BRING HER STUFF. WE COULD CARRY ENOUGH SUPPLIES FOR AN EXTENDED STAY.

YOU WANT TO GET A GROUP TOGETHER TO DRAW THE ROAMERS AWAY FROM THE WALL? I THOUGHT ABOUT THAT AS A LAST RESORT, BUT IT'S SO DANGEROUS...
THERE'S NO WAY YOU CAN GET A VEHICLE OUT OF HERE-- AND ON FOOT YOU'RE ONLY GOING TO BE ABLE TO DRAW A FEW ROAMERS TO YOU BEFORE YOU HAVE TO RETREAT, LEAVING SOME OF THEM AT THE WALL...
...I DON'T KNOW THAT IT'LL WORK.

MIGHT NOT BE PERFECT, BUT IT'S ALL WE'VE GOT, AND I FIGURED SINCE WE NEED TO GET SUPPLIES TO ANDREA *ANYWAY*, EVEN IF IT ONLY PULLS A FEW ROAMERS OFF THE WALLS IT'LL BE WORTH IT.

I CAN'T ARGUE WITH THAT... BUT HOW DO YOU PLAN ON GETTING OVER THE FENCE?
I HAVEN'T FIGURED THAT OUT YET. WAS GOING TO SEE IF HEATH HAD ANY IDEAS. SUN SHOULD BE UP IN A BIT... I'LL ASK HIM.

HEY, I THOUGHT YOU WERE GOING TO BRING CARL OVER THIS MORNING... THAT'S WHY I WAS UP... ONE REASON, AT LEAST.
NO, *UH*... JESSIE BROUGHT RON OVER LAST NIGHT, THEY WERE SCARED, SO THEY'RE STAYING IN THE HOUSE WITH US AND CARL'S WITH THEM.

JESSIE? WHICH ONE IS THAT? I HAVEN'T REALLY BEEN ABLE TO GET TO KNOW EVERYONE HERE, YET.

I DON'T BLAME YOU, THERE'S SO MANY PEOPLE. JUST THE OTHER DAY I MET A MAN WHO I SWEAR I'VE NEVER SEEN BEFORE.
IF I DIDN'T KNOW BETTER I'D SAY HE HAD SNUCK IN.

WAIT A MINUTE-- JESSIE? IS THAT PETE'S WIDOW?
HOW WELL DO YOU KNOW HER? YOU LEFT CARL WITH HER?

I KNOW HER WELL ENOUGH AND...
LOOK, CARL CAN TAKE CARE OF HIMSELF. I'M NOT WORRIED.

YOU'RE UP EARLY, SPENCER. WHAT'S GOT YOU OUT AND ABOUT?
OH, UH... IT'S ANDREA, ACTUALLY.

I KNEW HEATH HAD THIS MOUNTAIN CLIMBING ROPE AND RIG THAT HE'D FOUND. HE SAID HE WAS GOING TO USE IT IN THE CITY, TO GET UP INTO BUILDINGS TO LOOK FOR SUPPLIES WITHOUT HAVING TO DEAL WITH ALL THE WALKERS INSIDE.
BUT I FIGURED I COULD USE IT TO GET OVER THE FENCE TO ANDREA, GET HER SOME SUPPLIES.

WELL... MAGGIE'S PISSED AT ME. SHE UNDERSTANDS... BUT STILL... *PISSED.*
DENISE ISN'T TOO HAPPY EITHER... SOMETHING I'M GOING TO HAVE TO GET USED TO. IT'S WEIRD FOR ME. THIS IS THE FIRST RELATIONSHIP I'VE HAD SINCE THIS ALL STARTED.
DO WE REALLY NEED ALL THIS STUFF?
THESE PACKS ARE GETTING HEAVY, BUT YEAH, WE'RE PROBABLY GOING TO NEED ALL OF IT.

I'D GO WITH YOU BUT... I'M NOT GOING TO BE ABLE TO GET ACROSS THAT ROPE.

ACROSS IT? I WAS GOING TO USE IT TO SWING TO THE NEXT BUILDING... YOU THINK CLIMBING ACROSS WOULD BE EASIER?

NO BUILDINGS AROUND US HIGH ENOUGH TO SWING FROM THE ROPE. GONNA HAVE TO CLIMB ACROSS.
ONLY PROBLEM IS GOING TO BE GETTING THE OTHER END OF THE ROPE FIXED TO SOMETHING ON THE OTHER SIDE.

CLANKK!

DAMN.
AT LEAST I GOT IT ON THE ROOF, MAYBE I CAN SLING THE ROPE BETWEEN THE TWO PIPES FROM HERE. IF I DROP IT OFF THE ROOF AND HAVE TO PULL IT BACK... I'M NOT GETTING IT PAST ALL THE DEAD.
YOU THINK ANDREA CAN SEE US FROM HERE? I DON'T SEE HER IN THE TOWER.

ONE THING I'D FORGOTTEN SINCE THE PRISON... THE MOANING. HAVING THEM ON THE OTHER SIDE OF THE WALL LIKE THIS... THAT HORRIBLE SOUND.
YEAH.

JESUS. WHAT TIME IS IT? MY PATROL, THAT I NEVER EVEN STARTED, SHOULD BE OVER BY NOW.
JESSIE'S PROBABLY WONDERING WHERE THE HELL I AM.
GUYS...

...I GOT IT.
WE'RE ALL SET.

YEAH, SEEMS SECURE TO ME.
LOOKS LIKE THIS IS GOING TO WORK, YEAH. WE TAKING IT DOWN AFTER THEY GO UP?
NO, WE'RE KEEPING IT UP. MIGHT BE THEIR ONLY WAY BACK IN, IF THINGS GET UGLY. AND IF THINGS GET REALLY UGLY, COULD END UP BEING A GOOD ESCAPE ROUTE.
THAT'S WHAT I WAS THINKING...

MAGGIE, PLEASE... DON'T CRY. YOU JUST MAKE IT HARDER FOR ME.

CAN YOU TELL MY DAD THAT I... JUST...
TELL HIM NOT TO WORRY ABOUT ME.
I CAN DO THAT.

OKAY THEN.
DON'T CRY AND DON'T WORRY.

GIVE ME A MINUTE BEFORE YOU GO.
YEAH, SURE.

SO WHAT EXACTLY DO YOU HAVE IN MIND AFTER YOU'RE OUT THERE?
I'M GOING TO GET SUPPLIES TO ANDREA, MAKE SURE SHE'S OKAY AND THEN WE'RE GOING TO FORMULATE A PLAN TO ATTRACT THE ROAMERS AWAY FROM THE WALLS.
IT'S PRETTY SIMPLE.
BUT YOU DON'T HAVE THAT PLAN WORKED OUT ALREADY? I ONLY ASK BECAUSE...

BECAUSE YOU'RE WORRIED. I GET THAT, AND I AM, TOO. BUT YOU'RE JUST GOING TO HAVE TO TRUST ME.
ME, ANDREA, HEATH AND SPENCER... WE'RE SMART. WE'LL FIGURE SOMETHING OUT.
I THINK, MAYBE... JUST MAYBE, YOU DON'T GET TO SAVE US FROM THIS ONE YOURSELF, RICK.

AS WE GET TO THE MIDDLE... IT'S STARTING TO SAG MORE--WE SHOULD HAVE DONE THIS ONE AT A TIME.

SHIT!
RUH.

IT'S TOO MUCH WEIGHT!
GO BACK!

JUST KEEP GOING! IT DOESN'T HAVE A GOOD GRIP.

WE DON'T HAVE TIME FOR THAT--JUST KEEP MOVING. WE'VE ALREADY GOT TO WAIT FOR SPENCER. WHO KNOWS HOW LONG IT'LL TAKE US TO GET TO ANDREA IN THE TOWER.
I WANT TO GET THERE BEFORE DARK.

YEAH... THAT WENT GREAT!
OH, WE'RE-- UNGH-- FINE.

OKAY, MY TURN.

JUST A LITTLE MORE, MAN.
KEEP COMING, WE GOT YOU!

SNAP!
AAGH!

WRAMM!

OH, FUCK! GRAB THE ROPE! PULL HIM UP!
I'M PULLING!

GUYS?!
GUYS?!

FASTER!
UNGH!

AGGH!!

CAN'T--
I--

DID IT JUST--

JUST KEEP PULLING!

MY HANDS... JEEZ.
AND I LOST A DAMN SHOE. **CRAP.**

WELL, BOYS... GOOD PLAN SO FAR.
NOW WHAT?

SO WE'RE JUST SUPPOSED TO STAND HERE AND WATCH IT?
THAT'S ABOUT THE GIST OF IT, HOLLY. AS UNSETTLING AS IT IS.

DID THE PIECE NEXT TO IT JUST MOVE?

IT'S BEEN DOING THAT SINCE THE PANEL NEXT TO IT CAME LOOSE-- SWAYING LIKE THAT.

TRUCK'S THERE-- SHOULD HOLD THEM BOTH IF IT FALLS, TOO.
FUCK, TOBIN-- *LOOK!*

KROOM!

CHRIST!
SPLAKK!
I'LL HOLD THEM OFF! YOU GO WARN EVERYONE!

YOU CAN STAY HERE. IT'S NO PROBLEM. I LIKE HAVING YOU HERE.
CARL AND RON REALLY GET ALONG. UNTIL THIS BLOWS OVER, I THINK IT'LL BE GOOD FOR ALL OF US IF YOU--

RICK!
THE WALL IS DOWN!
SLAM!

LOCK THE DOORS, KEEP THE KIDS INSIDE AND AWAY FROM THE WINDOWS!
I'LL BE BACK AS SOON AS I CAN!

I'M GOING TO THE WALL. GET EVERYONE WITH A WEAPON OVER HERE... NO GUNS.
ABRAHAM, MORGAN, MICHONNE, NICHOLAS, WHOEVER YOU CAN FIND! TELL THEM TO BRING BATS, CROW BARS, AXES, WHATEVER THEY'VE GOT--NO GUNS! WE CAN'T DRAW ATTENTION TO THE FALLEN PART OF THE WALL.
GO!

JESUS.

GRUH.
GRAGGH.
GRRGH.

TOBIN...
DAMN.

SHIT!

WHERE'S MICHONNE?!
SHUKK!
DON'T KNOW!

HOLLY'S GOING TO TRY AND FIND HER. WHAT'S THE PLAN?!
WRAMM!

IF WE GET ENOUGH PEOPLE OVER HERE... WE CAN MANAGE THIS SITUATION--MIGHT EVEN BE EXACTLY WHAT WE NEEDED TO HAPPEN.
THEY TRICKLE IN, WE KEEP THEM CONTAINED, TAKE THEM OUT AS THEY COME THROUGH. WE CAN TAKE SHIFTS.
THIS COULD BE THE SAFEST WAY TO CLEAN THE WALLS OFF-- AT LEAST ENOUGH TO GO OUT THERE AND FINISH THE JOB.

WE JUST-- NEED TO HAVE ENOUGH PEOPLE HERE!
SHUKK!

WRAMM!
DAMN, THEY'RE COMING IN FAST!
THERE'S TOO MANY OF THEM!

YEEAAAAGGH!!
GRAGGH!

NO! GET UP! YOU CAN'T JUST GIVE UP!
C'MON-- MOVE!

MORGAN--
DAMN IT!

NO!
I DON'T WANT TO DIE!

YOU DON'T HAVE TO IF YOU GET UP!
C'MON!
GRAAAGH!
RUGHL.

OKAY, OKAY... I'M UP--I'M GETTING UP.
WRAAM!

MORGAN!
I'M OKAY-- I'M--

MICHONNE, WAIT!
WE GOTTA TAKE HIS ARM OFF--IT'S THE ONLY THING THAT COULD SAVE HIM.

WRAMMM!

MY ARM? WHAT DO YOU--?

YEAAGH!
SHASH!!

HOLD ON THERE-- I GOT YOU!

WE'LL GET YOU PATCHED UP--COME ON!

SVAASH!
GET HIM OUT OF HERE!

TRYING TO.

SVAASSH!

OH, FUCK!

THORKK!!

GET HIM TO SAFETY. WE GOT THIS.

MORGAN! HANG IN THERE!
I CAN'T CARRY YOU ALONE.
RICK!

THRAKK!

WHAT ARE YOU DOING?
THE DOCTOR'S PLACE IS THAT WAY!

TOO FAR, HE'S LOST TOO MUCH BLOOD ALREADY. MY PLACE-- PATCH HIM UP.
DENISE CAN COME TO US.

CAN YOU SEE ANYTHING? I CAN'T TELL IF ANYONE'S OUT THERE... ALL I SEE IS THE ROAMERS.
IT'S TOO FAR AWAY, I JUST SEE THE WALL SPLITTING AND THE ROAMERS PILING IN...
JESUS.

THERE'S NOTHING WE CAN DO RIGHT NOW... IT'D TAKE ALL NIGHT TO GET TO THEM.
THEY'RE JUST TOO DAMN FAR.
WE'RE ALL GOING TO DIE.

I'M SORRY, IT'S JUST... IT'S NEVER BEEN THIS BAD, NOT BEFORE... NOT EVER. THIS IS... BAD.
I JUST CAN'T SHAKE THE FEELING THAT THINGS DON'T END WELL FOR US. MAYBE NOT ALL OF US... BUT ME FOR SURE.
I HAVEN'T BEEN ABLE TO SLEEP... I JUST DON'T FEEL... NORMAL. I DON'T KNOW WHAT IT IS. I HAVE A SICK FEELING.
I DON'T SEE MY LIFE AFTER THIS... I JUST CAN'T... PICTURE IT IN MY HEAD WHEN I THINK ABOUT IT.

I'M NOT GOING TO SURVIVE THIS.
I KNOW IT.

SHLUKK!
KEEP MOVING! DON'T LET THEM GET BEHIND US!

WE'RE LOSING GROUND HERE!
THERE'S TOO DAMN MANY!
SHUKK!

ROSITA AND EUGENE ARE GETTING EVERYONE ELSE!
WRUKK!
WE JUST HAVE TO HOLD OUT A LITTLE *LONGER!* WE GET EVERYONE OUT HERE--AND WE'LL KILL 'EM FASTER THAN THEY'RE GETTING IN!

FUCK!
WRAKK!

FUCK!
KRAK!

FUCK!
WRAMM!!

DON'T GET SO WORKED UP, KILLER. YOU'RE GOING TO GIVE YOURSELF A HEART ATTACK.

OKAY, IT'S PRETTY OBVIOUS WHAT WE'RE DOING HERE, PEOPLE--
IF IT'S DEAD-- FUCKING KILL IT!

GRUH.
GAK!

THERE'S TOO MANY--
--TOO GOD DAMN MANY OF THEM!!
KRAKK!

WELL?
WELL... THAT'S ALL I CAN DO. HE'S PATCHED UP. HE'S LOST A LOT OF BLOOD, BUT THERE'S REALLY NOTHING ELSE THAT CAN BE DONE.
THERE'S NO WAY OF KNOWING IF THE ARM WAS TAKEN OFF FAST ENOUGH... NOT YET.
SO WE *WAIT*.

HE SHOULD BE AWAKE SOON. HE'LL BE WEAK, BUT AS LONG AS THE BITE DIDN'T INFECT HIM, HE'LL BE OKAY.
YOU PRAY?

NOT REALLY. NO.
NOTHING YOU CAN DO EITHER, THEN. SORRY.

HE OKAY?
DON'T KNOW YET.

MORGAN... YOU'RE A DAMN *FOOL*.

CAN YOU TAKE ME BACK OVER TO MY PLACE? I BET THEY DON'T HAVE THE WALKERS CLEANED UP YET.

YEAH, CAN YOU GO **NOW?** I NEED TO GET OUT THERE AND HELP.
DO YOU HAVE YOUR--
KNOCK! KNOCK! KNOCK!

LOCK THE DOOR!
TURN OFF THE LIGHTS!
STAY AWAY FROM THE WINDOWS!

WHAT IS IT, MAGGIE?!

JUST LOOK OUTSIDE.

BACK!
GOD DAMN IT, GET--
FUCK!

FUCK IT!
GET TO YOUR HOUSES, EVERYONE! GET--

ROSITA?!
HOLLY?!

IT'S TOO LATE! THEY'RE GETTING PAST EVERYONE!

COME ON-- LET'S GET BACK TO THE HOUSE.
DID YOU SEE ANYONE ELSE? HOLLY MAKE IT?

SAW EUGENE RUNNING AWAY...
THAT'S IT.

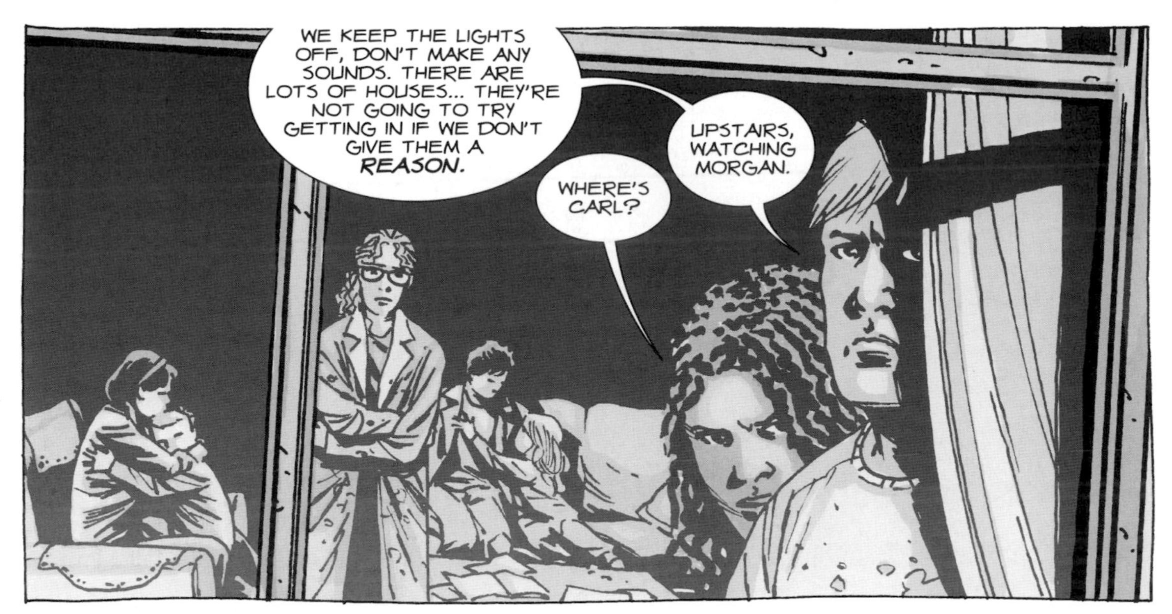
WE KEEP THE LIGHTS OFF, DON'T MAKE ANY SOUNDS. THERE ARE LOTS OF HOUSES... THEY'RE NOT GOING TO TRY GETTING IN IF WE DON'T GIVE THEM A *REASON*.
WHERE'S CARL?
UPSTAIRS, WATCHING MORGAN.

YOU THINK I DON'T KNOW WHAT THAT MEANS?

...
I NEED TO GET BACK TO MY HOUSE. IF SOMEONE'S HURT--THAT'S WHERE THEY'LL GO...

UNNGH.
CRAP!

YOU'RE NOT GOING TO NEED THAT, I DON'T THINK.

YEAH...
SORRY.

SO THEY GOT YOU... WATCHING ME, MAKING SURE I DON'T TURN?
YEAH.
I CAN DO IT... I'M OLD ENOUGH.

I KNOW... I KNOW...
HOW OLD ARE YOU, CARL?

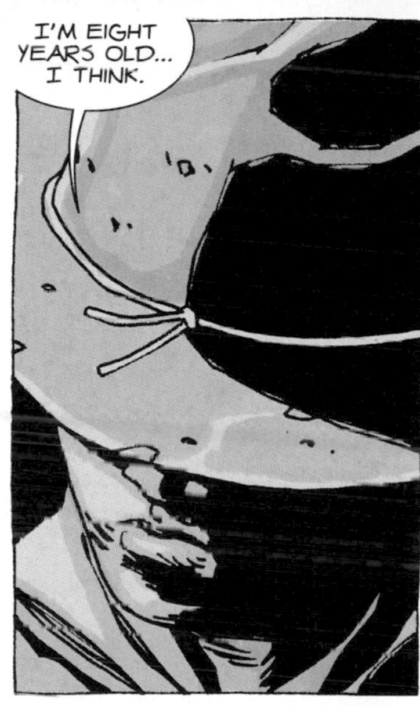
I'M EIGHT YEARS OLD... I THINK.

YOU THINK?
THEY SKIPPED MY BIRTHDAY, I'M PRETTY SURE. IT'S WINTER AGAIN... BUT I NEVER HAD ONE.
IT'S IN APRIL.

I'M SORRY... TO HEAR THAT...
HAD A BIRTHDAY PARTY FOR MY SON DUANE... SHORTLY AFTER CHRISTMAS... BEFORE HE...

...
CARL... I SAW YOU SHOOT BEN.

I KNOW YOU DID.

I HAVE DONE THIS... THIS IS ALL MY FAULT.
WE ARE ALL GOING TO DIE.

REGINA..

I'M SORRY.

AND WHAT KIND OF PERSON AM I...
...TO WISH YOU WERE HERE WITH ME?

WRAMM! WRAMM! WRAMM!

WRAMM! WRAMM! WRAMM!

GOD DAMN IT, GABRIEL!
OPEN UP! WE'RE GOING TO *DIE!*
OPEN--!

QUICKLY!
COME ON!

HURRY!!

HOW LONG DID I--?
IT'S MORNING. WE MADE IT THROUGH THE NIGHT WITHOUT SO MUCH AS A TAP ON THE WINDOW. WOULD HAVE WOKE ME, I'M A LIGHT SLEEPER.
WHERE'S CARL?

YOU SAT DOWN FOR A MINUTE, DOZED OFF. I GOT THEM BOTH OFF TO BED, THEY'RE STILL ASLEEP.
THEY HAVEN'T... SEEN US.

GOOD, OKAY. I JUST DON'T WANT THINGS TO BE WEIRD HERE. WE MIGHT ALL NEED TO *STAY* IN THIS HOUSE AND...
I GET IT. I CERTAINLY DON'T WANT TO EXPLAIN THIS TO RON.

I REALLY LIKE HAVING YOU HERE.

HE OKAY?
FEVER'S BAD. HE'S WEAK... OKAY, FOR NOW.
I'M DYING, OKAY?! I KNOW IT, YOU KNOW IT. THE ARM DIDN'T COME OFF SOON ENOUGH.
LET'S ALL JUST STOP KIDDING OURSELVES.

DON'T SAY THAT. COULD BE ANYTHING GIVING YOU A FEVER.
DAMN IT, MORGAN.

OKAY, I KNOW... I'M SORRY.
CAN YOU GIVE ME A MINUTE WITH CARL? I WANT TO TALK TO HIM.

OKAY, I'LL... BE RIGHT OUTSIDE.
UM... OKAY.

CARL, I...
WHAT I SAW YOU DO... I WANTED TO TALK TO YOU ABOUT THAT. YOU'RE... A REMARKABLE YOUNG MAN, CARL. YOU REMIND ME A LOT OF MY SON DUANE.
I'M SORRY THAT YOU NEVER GOT TO MEET HIM.
YOU DID WHAT YOU... DID FOR A REASON. YOU KNEW IT WAS WHAT NEEDED TO BE DONE, BUT NOBODY ELSE COULD DO IT.

SO YOU KILLED THAT BOY. AND IT AFFECTED YOU... I SAW THAT.

YOU'RE NO COLD-BLOODED KILLER. I SAW YOU AWAKE NIGHTS... SAW HOW IT HURT YOU TO HAVE TO DO THAT.
YEAH...

YOU--
COUGH! COUGH!

YOU'RE A GOOD BOY. DON'T LET ANYONE TAKE THAT AWAY FROM YOU-- DON'T EVER LET YOURSELF THINK DIFFERENTLY. YOU CARE ABOUT PEOPLE.
THAT'S EASY TO LOSE... CARING ABOUT PEOPLE.
WE GET SO FOCUSED ON WHAT WE NEED... WE STOP CARING ABOUT OTHER PEOPLE. MAYBE IT'S WHAT WE HAVE TO DO TO GET BY...
...BUT IT TAKES AWAY A PIECE OF YOUR SOUL... EVERY TIME.

I--
HAKK!
I KNOW-- THE THINGS I'VE DONE...

YOU'RE EIGHT YEARS OLD. YOU'RE QUICKLY HITTING THE AGE WHERE YOU START TO BECOME THE PERSON YOU'RE GOING TO BE.
THESE ARE IMPORTANT TIMES, SON.

YOU JUST DON'T KNOW HOW MUCH IT HURTS ME TO THINK ABOUT THE THINGS THIS WORLD IS GOING TO **DENY** YOU.
ARE YOU LISTENING TO ME?
Y--YES.
YOUR INNOCENCE... THAT'S **LOST.** GONE, JUST--

COUGH!
HAKK!

SCHOOL... WHAT YOU LEARN FROM IT... WHAT YOU **REALLY** LEARN FROM IT. NOT THE NONSENSE IN THE BOOK...
...HOW THE WORLD WORKS. HOW PEOPLE INTERACT... LIFE STUFF.

YOU **NEED** THAT STUFF. IT'S IMPORTANT.
I DON'T KNOW HOW YOU'LL BE, HERE ON YOUR OWN WITHOUT ME. NO ONE TO TALK TO...
...AND AFTER I'M GONE...

...YOU'RE GOING TO HAVE TO BE **STRONG,** DUANE.

I'M NOT DUANE.
HE'S **DEAD.**

HE... HE IS.
OH, GOD...

WE DRIVE A CAR INTO THEM--AND IT JUST GETS STUCK DRIVING OVER THEM--AND IT'S SWARMED. WE SET THEM ON FIRE, THEY COULD BURN HOUSES DOWN, AND WHO KNOWS HOW LONG THAT WOULD TAKE TO KILL THEM.
I DON'T KNOW WHAT TO DO.
A GOOD QUARTER OF THOSE ROAMERS AT THE WALL HAVE ALREADY FILTERED INSIDE--AND MORE GET IN EVERY MINUTE... THEY'RE CLIMBING OVER EACH OTHER--AND THAT'S SLOWING THEM DOWN...
BUT THEY'RE IN, SO WHAT CAN WE DO ANYWAY?

WHO SAYS WE HAVE TO DO ANYTHING?
MAYBE WE JUST GO? WE LEAVE THEM.

LEAVE THEM?!
ARE YOU JOKING? GLENN'S GOT A KID IN THERE, AND MAGGIE. HE'S NOT GOING TO LEAVE THEM BEHIND.
WHAT ABOUT YOUR DAD?
MY FATHER MIGHT AS WELL HAVE DIED WHEN MY MOTHER DID. HAVE YOU SEEN HIM?
AND WHO SAYS GLENN OR HEATH COME? WE COULD GO... JUST YOU AND ME.

WRAMM!

SO THAT'S ABOUT THE END OF "YOU AND ME."
WHAT WAS THAT?!
WHAT HAPPENED?!

WHAT'S IT DOING?!
JUST STANDING THERE--IT TAPPED ON THE WINDOW A MINUTE AGO. I DON'T THINK IT KNOWS WE'RE IN HERE.

GOD DAMN IT. IT'S GOING TO DRAW MORE OF THEM ON THE PORCH--IT MAY NOT THINK WE'RE IN HERE...
...OTHERS WILL.

MOMMY, I'M SCARED.

DON'T BE SCARED, SOPHIA. WE'RE GONNA BE FINE.
YOU'LL SEE.

WE CAN'T STAY HERE.
THINGS ARE ONLY GOING TO GET WORSE. THEY'RE STILL PRETTY THIN IN THE STREETS, WE COULD MAKE IT TO THE GATE, MAYBE PUSH THROUGH THEM...
I DON'T LIKE THE IDEA, BUT I CAN'T KEEP YOU ALL SAFE HERE... NOT FOR LONG.
...MAKE A RUN FOR IT.
YOU MEAN... LEAVE EVERYONE ELSE?

THE FENCE IS DOWN, JESSIE. I CAN'T GET TO THEM--EVEN IF I COULD... WHAT WOULD I DO? LEAD MORE PEOPLE OUT--THROUGH THE MASSES?
THEY'D PICK US OFF--IT'D SLOW US DOWN TOO MUCH. A SMALL GROUP WOULD BE FINE. JUST US... ONCE WE'RE OUT WE CAN FIGURE OUT HOW TO HELP THE REST.

WE CAN'T LEAVE THEM HERE--NOT UNTIL WE... FIGURE SOMETHING OUT.
THERE ARE FAMILIES HERE... CHILDREN.

I KNOW, BUT WHAT CHOICE DO WE HAVE?
THE THING TO KEEP IN MIND... ABOUT OTHER PEOPLE'S CHILDREN...

...THEY'RE NOT OUR CHILDREN.

I DON'T MEAN TO SOUND SO INSENSITIVE... BUT IF I HAVE TO CHOOSE BETWEEN MY CHILD OR SOMEONE ELSE'S CHILD...
I'M GOING TO CHOOSE MINE **EVERY** SINGLE TIME.

I'M SORRY, I'M JUST BEING **HONEST.**

ONCE **WE'RE** OUT... WE'LL FIND A WAY TO HELP EVERYONE ELSE?

YES, OF COURSE.
WE WOULDN'T JUST **ABANDON** EVERYONE.

OKAY THEN. LET'S GATHER SUPPLIES, AS MUCH AS WE CAN CARRY WITHOUT SLOWING US DOWN...
...AND LET'S GET OUT OF HERE WHILE WE STILL **CAN.**

I'M SORRY I'M SUCH A BITCH. I DON'T MEAN TO BE, IT'S JUST... IT'S THE WAY I AM.
I DIDN'T MEAN TO SAY THOSE THINGS TO YOU, I WISH I COULD TAKE IT BACK NOW. GET OVER THE DEATH OF YOUR SON? MOVE ON?
SOMETIMES I LISTEN TO MYSELF AND... I JUST DON'T KNOW.

TRUTH IS, YOUR STRENGTH, HOW YOU CARRIED ON AFTER LOSING YOUR SON... IT'S WHAT FIRST ATTRACTED ME TO YOU.
YOU WERE A BROKEN MAN, WITH EVERY REASON TO GIVE UP, BUT YOU DIDN'T. YOU PRESSED ON.
I KNEW I HAD A THING FOR YOU THE SECOND I LAID EYES ON YOU.

BUT I JUST CAN'T BE *NICE.*
I CAN'T JUST EXPRESS HOW I *FEEL*... LIKE THAT WOULD SOMEHOW BE TOO REVEALING... LEAVING ME... *EXPOSED.*

SO I FAKE BEING COOL, I HIDE MY TRUE EMOTIONS... I TRY TO BE COLD, CALM AND COLLECTED.
I HAVE TROUBLE OPENING UP TO PEOPLE.

AND NOW HERE WE ARE.
MORGAN, YOU NEED TO KNOW HOW MUCH I TRULY CARE ABOUT YOU. I REALLY DID, NO MATTER HOW I MAY HAVE ACTED.
CAN YOU EVER FORGIVE ME?

MORGAN?

RICK, STOP.
WHAT IS IT?

I'M NOT GOING.
I'M STAYING HERE WITH SOPHIA.

BUT MAGGIE, WHY? YOU KNOW IT'S NOT SAFE TO STAY HERE.

I'M NOT FAST, NEVER HAVE BEEN. SAME WITH SOPHIA.. WE CAN'T GET OUT OF HERE, NOT ON FOOT, NOT PUSHING THROUGH THE DEAD.
I JUST DON'T FEEL RIGHT. THEY'LL GET US, I KNOW IT.
I CAN'T RISK SOPHIA'S LIFE LIKE THAT. I JUST CAN'T.

YEAH, YOU MIGHT NOT BE FAST ENOUGH. NONE OF US ARE. I ACTUALLY HAD AN IDEA ON THAT.
IS THAT ROAMER STILL ON THE PORCH?

YEAH, WHY?

OH, MY GOD!

DON'T WORRY.
I'VE DONE THIS *BEFORE.*

YOU SHOULD TAKE THE KIDS TO ANOTHER ROOM.

IT'S OKAY, ROSITA. WE'LL BE SAFE IN HERE.
JUST HOLD ME... I CAN'T STOP SHAKING.

LORD, PLEASE... DELIVER US FROM--
THOSE DOORS ARE SOLID, GABRIEL. THEY'RE NOT GETTING IN HERE. I PROMISE.
NICHOLAS AND I ARE STARVING, YOU GOT ANYTHING TO EAT?

THERE WERE SO MANY OF THEM... DO YOU THINK THEY SAW US COME IN HERE?
THEY'D BE TEARING THIS PLACE DOWN BY NOW IF THEY HAD. I THINK WE'RE FINE, ERIC.

C-C-C--
I CAN'T--

OKAY, SPENCER AND I WILL TAKE THIS STREET, GLENN AND HEATH, YOU'RE ONE STREET OVER. KEEP THEM AS CLOSE TO YOU AS POSSIBLE, DON'T GET TOO FAR AWAY, LURE AS MANY WITH YOU AS YOU CAN.
WE'LL MEET UP SIX BLOCKS DOWN AND LOSE THEM... THEN WE COME BACK, AND START IT AGAIN.
WE KEEP DOING THIS, WE'LL THIN THEM OUT-- AS LONG AS NOTHING HAPPENS TO DRAW THEM BACK.

I'M SORRY, MORGAN.

THUNK!
OH, MY GOD--WHAT ARE YOU *DOING?!*

I KNOW IT LOOKS BAD, BUT THIS WILL ACTUALLY KEEP THEM OFF US. THEY'LL THINK WE'RE DEAD LIKE THEM.
IT WORKED BEFORE.
KEEP RIPPING THOSE SHEETS, WE'RE GOING TO TURN THEM INTO PONCHOS FOR EVERYONE.

MICHONNE...?

MORGAN IS DEAD.

WHAT CAN I DO TO HELP?

I'M JUST GOING TO MY INFIRMARY, AND I DON'T KNOW WHO OR WHAT IS WAITING FOR ME THERE--I CAN'T COVER MYSELF WITH THAT CRAP.
I CAN HELP YOU GET THERE WITHOUT IT.
I KNOW IT WORKED BEFORE, GLENN TOLD ME ALL ABOUT IT... BUT WE'RE STILL NOT GOING. I CAN'T TAKE THE RISK.
WE'RE GOING TO STAY.

MAGGIE, IT'S ONLY A MATTER OF TIME BEFORE THEY--OKAY... YOU'VE MADE UP YOUR MIND, I DON'T HAVE TIME TO CONVINCE YOU.
I HOPE YOU'RE DOING THE RIGHT THING.

YOU READY?
I AM. I'D FOLLOW YOU ANYWHERE.

BYE, CARL.
YEAH. BYE.

REMEMBER, PUT AS MUCH AS YOU CAN ON YOUR SHOULDERS, SO IT DOESN'T SLIDE OFF--SMEAR SOME PARTS OVER YOUR CHEST AND BACK... COVER AS MUCH AREA AS YOU CAN...
OKAY, LET'S ALL GET SUITED UP. IT'S NOW OR NEVER.

STICK TOGETHER AND MOVE SLOWLY. JUST STAY CALM AND WE'LL BE FINE.
I THINK DENISE IS DRAWING ATTENTION-- I'M TAKING HER ON AHEAD.

I WAS RIGHT, THEY'RE REALLY THINNING OUT IN FRONT OF THE GATE AS THEY SPILL INSIDE, IF WE CAN GET THAT GATE OPEN WITHOUT ATTRACTING THEM TO US--WE'RE HOME FREE.

RON, COME ON...
RON?

RICK...

C'MON, DOUGLAS... YOU KNOW THIS IS THE ONLY WAY.

ALMOST THERE-- KEEP MOVING.
UFF!

JUST KEEP MOVING. IGNORE IT.

MOM, I'M SCARED!
I WANT TO GO BACK!

STOP TALKING-- WE CAN'T GO BACK.
C'MON!

STOP.
NOW.
YOU'RE DRAWING ATTENTION.

AAAGH!
RON!

DAMN IT! YOU'RE ALMOST THERE--RUN! YOU CAN MAKE IT ON YOUR OWN.
DON'T LEAVE ME!

MOMMY!!
AAAGH!

YOU HAVE TO LEAVE HIM! THERE'S NOTHING WE CAN DO FOR HIM NOW! LET GO OF HIS HAND!
JESSIE!

I CAN'T LEAVE HIM!

THAT'S IT... THAT--

RICK!

RIIIICK!!

DON'T LEAVE US!

DAD-- SHE WON'T LET GO!
DAD, THEY'RE GOING TO GET ME!

DAD!

I'M SORRY.

DON'T-- LEAVE-- US--!

THUNK!
AAAGH!

THUKK!

BLAM!!
RICK!

GET BACK INSIDE! YOU'LL BE SAFE IN THE HOUSES! GO!
BLAM!

STOP SHOOTING!
STOP!
YOU'LL DRAW MORE OF THEM TO US!

DON'T LOOK OUTSIDE, HONEY.
IGNORE THE SCREAMS...

IS ANYONE IN HERE?! I'M BACK!
HELLO?!

GET TO SAFETY!
I'LL COVER YOU!
BLAM!

STOP FIRING THAT GODDAMN GUN!
THUNK!

NNGH.
GRARGH!

GOD DAMN IT!

THUKK!

BLAM! BLAM!

BLAM!

BLAM!

BLAM!

IS EVERYONE--?

DAD?

DU--

CARL!

WRAMM!

GOD--
THANK GOD.

WHUDD!

KEEP BREATHING, CARL.
JUST KEEP BREATHING!

SHRIPP!

KEEP BREATHING...

RICK?!
WHAT HAPPENED?!

WHUDD!

DENISE!
OPEN!
WRAMM!

OH, MY GOD!

PLEASE.
SAVE HIS LIFE!

PLEASE.
CARL'S ALL I HAVE LEFT...

COME IN!
PUT HIM ON THE BED!

I'VE GOT TO USE THE LIGHTS, ELECTRICITY-- IT'S NOT GOING TO BE QUIET, IT'S GOING TO DRAW A LOT OF ATTENTION.
BUT I'LL...
I'LL DO EVERYTHING I CAN.

DO WHATEVER YOU HAVE TO DO--I'LL HOLD THEM BACK.
JUST DON'T LET HIM DIE!

RICK, I DON'T--

DON'T LET HIM DIE!

GRUH.

WRAMM!

THOKK!

SHLUK!

KRAK!

WRAMM!

SHUNK!

WRAMM!

THUNK!

WHAT THE FUCK ARE THEY DOING?!

THEY'RE SHOOTING GUNS IN THERE NOW?

IT STOPPED, BUT YEAH... SOMETHING MUST HAVE--
WE NEED TO MOVE.

WE SHOULD MEET UP WITH GLENN AND HEATH, MAYBE THEY'RE HAVING MORE LUCK.
AND CALM DOWN, MOST OF THE ROAMERS ARE AT THE FENCE--OR INSIDE IT. AVOIDING THESE STRAGGLERS IS CAKE.

I'M JUST NOT USED TO BEING OUT HERE.
IT'S UNSETTLING.

HEH.
YEAH.

WHAT ARE YOU DOING HERE?! WE'RE SUPPOSED TO LURE THEM DOWN PARALLEL STREETS!

WE ONLY LURED A FEW AWAY, GUNSHOTS DREW BACK ALL THE ONES THAT COULDN'T LOOK RIGHT AT US.

SAME HERE-- BUT I THINK WE STARTED WITH MORE THAN YOU DID.

WOW, YEAH...

SO THOSE GUNSHOTS-- THAT WAS FROM *INSIDE?*
WHAT IF WE JUST SHOOT OUT HERE? DRAW THEM BACK?

COULD BE TOO DANGEROUS. DON'T KNOW WHAT HAPPENED IN THERE...
LET'S PUT MORE DISTANCE BETWEEN US AND THEM, SO WE CAN TALK.
COME ON.

SHUKK!

SWASSH!

IS CARL OKAY?!
HE HAS TO BE!

STOP BLEEDING!
GOD DAMN IT, STOP BLEEDING!

SVASSH!
WHUKK!

RICK...?

PLEASE, I KNOW IT'S DANGEROUS-- JUST... HELP ME.
WHAKK!

OH, MY GOD-- ABRAHAM, LOOK OUTSIDE.
WHAT IS IT?

WHUKK!

I CAN'T JUST LEAVE THEM OUT THERE.
NO! YOU CAN'T HELP THEM! THERE'S TOO MANY!

SVAASH!

SOMETHING IS DRAWING THEM AWAY FROM US--I THINK I SEE A SWORD MOVING IN THE MIDDLE OF THE SWARM.
SOMEONE IS ABOUT TO DIE...

SHUNK!

I'M GOING TO HELP THEM. I WON'T JUST LEAVE THEM TO DIE!
AARON, WAIT! I'M NOT GOING TO LET YOU DO IT ALONE!

SVAASH!

WHAT THE HELL?

OVER HERE, YOU UNDEAD FUCKWADS!

GRUH.

WRAMM!

HUFF!
HUFF!
HUFF!
WHAT HAPPENED?
ABRAHAM.

DAMN IT!

I KNOW I'M GOING TO REGRET THIS.

THERE'S-- NOTHING TO SEE. LET MOMMY LOOK.
YOU SIT TIGHT.

C'MON, GABRIEL. YOU CAN'T SIT THIS ONE OUT.
YOU CAN'T BE SCARED, YOU'RE NOT ALLOWED... WE NEED YOU, MAN!

WHAT ARE THEY DOING?!
THUKK!

THEY'RE COMING TO HELP!
SVASSH!

WRAMM!!

IT'S SIMPLE MATH, WE EACH KILL TEN... AND THIS IS PRETTY MUCH OVER.
WE CAN DO THIS.
WHAKK!

WHUDD!

LORD, GIVE ME STRENGTH.
WRAKK!

SVASSH!

THERE'S SO GODDAMN MANY OF THEM!
WROKK!

SHUKK!

WE GOTTA HOLD THE LINE--THIS TIME, WE CAN'T GIVE IN!
KRAKK!

WRAKK!

WRAMM!

KRAK!

HUFF!
HUFF!
WRAKK!

IT'S STARTING TO THIN OUT--KEEP IT UP!

I CAN'T--
I CAN'T BELIEVE THIS...

GO TAKE A BREAK--I'LL COVER YOU.
NO!

I'M OKAY...

THIS IS A STORY PEOPLE ARE GOING TO TELL. I'M A PART OF THIS-- I'M NOT GIVING UP.
C'MON!

CARL... GOD DAMN IT...
FOCUS ON THIS! WE'RE THINNING THEM OUT--BUT WE'RE NOT OUT OF THE WOODS YET.
DON'T LET YOURSELF GET DISTRACTED.

OH, GOD-- SOMETHING IS HAPPENING IN THERE, DO YOU HEAR THEM?
SOMETHING'S GOT ALL THE ROAMERS INSIDE RILED UP-- THEY'RE IN A FRENZY.
OH, GOD, NO...

WRAKK!

SKRAGG!

WHAKK!

WRAMM!

WROKK!

SVAASH!

SHUKK!

HUFF!
HUFF!
THEY'RE STILL SPILLING IN THROUGH THE BREAK IN THE FENCE... THIS AIN'T OVER YET.

LET THEM COME--TAKE A BREATHER AND THEN WE'LL DEAL WITH THEM.

AND THEN WHAT?

WE *REBUILD.*
THIS IS OUR HOME NOW. WE WILL CLEAN IT UP, REPAIR THE WALLS... AND CARRY ON.
WE'RE NOT GOING ANYWHERE.

I'VE GOT TO--
GO ON, WE'VE GOT THIS COVERED FROM HERE.

FUCK THE BREATHER... FOLLOW ME.

OKAY, PEOPLE-- WE'RE IN THE HOME STRETCH! LET'S FUCKING DAMN WELL SLEEP GOOD TONIGHT!
WRAMM!

SHAASH!

WHAKK!

GUYS.
LOOK.
WHUDD!

OH, MY GOD! WE HEARD SHOTS AND FEARED FOR THE WORST!
IT'S THINNED OUT SO MUCH THAT WE CAN MOVE FREELY AND PICK THEM OFF-- THERE'S MAYBE A COUPLE DOZEN LEFT OUT THERE!
AND YOU GUYS CLEANED OUT INSIDE?!
I CAN'T BELIEVE THIS!

I CAN'T BELIEVE IT TOOK ME THIS LONG TO REALIZE THIS. AFTER SO LONG, BEING DRIVEN FROM ONE PLACE TO THE NEXT... I NOTICED, IT WAS ALWAYS PEOPLE--THAT WAS THE PROBLEM.
I CAN'T BELIEVE I'M SAYING THIS... BUT THE DEAD...
THEY'RE A MANAGEABLE THREAT.
I SEE THE MISTAKE I MADE, WANTING TO RUN... NOT BEING WILLING TO STAND AND FIGHT... IT COST JESSIE AND RON THEIR LIVES. I HAVE TO LIVE WITH THAT...
BUT I'VE SEEN WHAT WE CAN DO WITH NUMBERS. I'VE SEEN HOW WE CAN ORGANIZE, PLAN... HOW IF WE DO THINGS RIGHT... IF EVERYONE DOES THEIR PART... WE CAN SURVIVE ANYTHING.
THIS PLACE IS OURS, THE FENCE, THE HOUSES--WE CAN MAKE THIS A HOME. WE'VE BEEN LAZY UP UNTIL NOW... BUT THAT ALL CHANGES, TODAY--THIS INSTANT.
I SEE NOW WHAT WE CAN DO, WITH ENOUGH PEOPLE, WITH A STRATEGY... WE CAN MAKE THIS PLACE MUCH MORE SAFE... SECURE.
WE CAN SET UP ROADBLOCKS--SURROUND THIS PLACE WITH A MAZE FOR THE DEAD, KEEPING THEM OFF THE WALLS IN SIGNIFICANT NUMBERS.
WE CAN REBUILD THE WALLS, STRONGER, TALLER... MAKE OUR COMMUNITY BETTER THAN IT EVER WAS.

OUR PEOPLE NEED TO BE TRAINED--BETTER EQUIPPED TO DEAL WITH ANYTHING THAT COULD HAPPEN--WE'LL NEED TO INVEST IN TRAINING AND PREPAREDNESS.
WE'LL TURN OURSELVES INTO AN ARMY THAT CAN PROTECT US.

I SEE THIS... ALL OF THIS HAPPENING, IT'S ALL POSSIBLE. IT'S JUST SO... *CLEAR* TO ME.
I SEE OUR SHORTCOMINGS, THAT LED US TO COWER IN OUR HOUSES AT THE SIGHT OF ROAMERS IN THE STREETS... AND I SEE HOW TO *ELIMINATE* THEM.

I THINK ABOUT THE ROAD AHEAD OF US, AND FOR THE FIRST TIME IT SEEMS LONG... AND BRIGHT.

AFTER EVERYTHING WE'VE BEEN THROUGH, ALL THE PEOPLE WE'VE LOST... I SUDDENLY FIND MYSELF OVERCOME WITH SOMETHING I THOUGHT WE'D LOST...

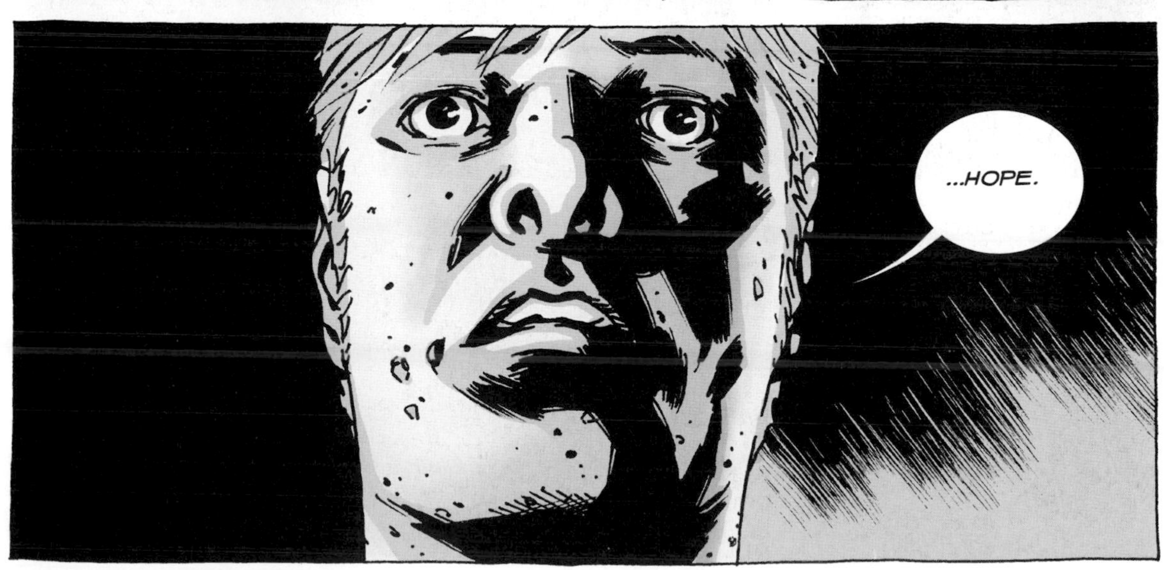
...HOPE.

I WANT TO SHOW YOU THIS NEW WORLD. I WANT TO MAKE IT A REALITY FOR YOU.
PLEASE, CARL--LIVE SO THAT I CAN SHOW YOU.

PLEASE.

TO BE CONTINUED...

MORE GREAT BOOKS FROM ROBERT KIRKMAN & IMAGE COMICS!

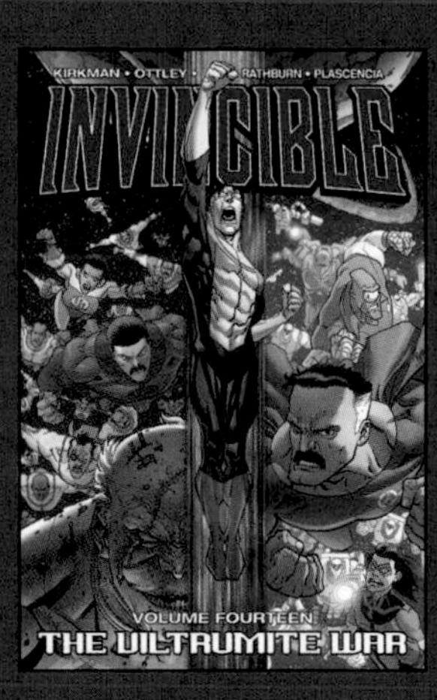

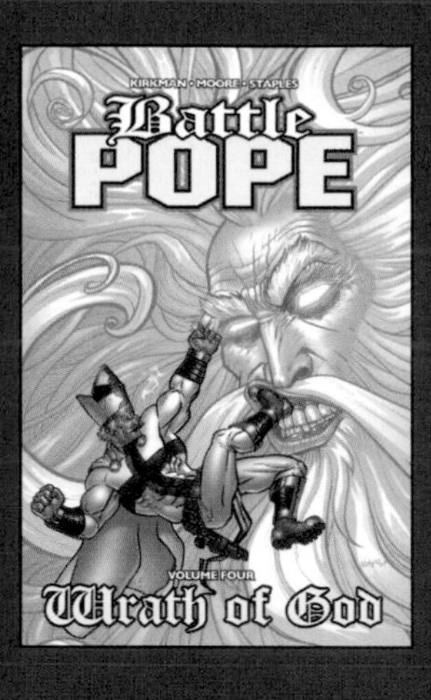

THE ASTOUNDING WOLF-MAN

VOL. 1 TP
ISBN: 978-1-58240-862-0
$14.99

VOL. 2 TP
ISBN: 978-1-60706-007-9
$14.99

VOL. 3 TP
ISBN: 978-1-60706-111-3
$16.99

VOL. 4 TP
ISBN: 978-1-60706-249-3
$16.99

BATTLE POPE

VOL. 1: GENESIS TP
ISBN: 978-1-58240-572-8
$14.99

VOL. 2: MAYHEM TP
ISBN: 978-1-58240-529-2
$12.99

VOL. 3: PILLOW TALK TP
ISBN: 978-1-58240-677-0
$12.99

VOL. 4: WRATH OF GOD TP
ISBN: 978-1-58240-751-7
$9.99

BRIT

VOL. 1: OLD SOLDIER TP
ISBN: 978-1-58240-678-7
$14.99

VOL. 2: AWOL
ISBN: 978-1-58240-864-4
$14.99

VOL. 3: FUBAR
ISBN: 978-1-60706-061-1
$16.99

CAPES

VOL. 1: PUNCHING THE CLOCK TP
ISBN: 978-1-58240-756-2
$17.99

HAUNT

VOL. 1 TP
ISBN: 978-1-60706-154-0
$9.99

VOL. 2 TP
ISBN: 978-1-60706-229-5
$16.99

INVINCIBLE

VOL. 1: FAMILY MATTERS TP
ISBN: 978-1-58240-711-1
$12.99

VOL. 2: EIGHT IS ENOUGH TP
ISBN: 978-1-58240-347-2
$12.99

VOL. 3: PERFECT STRANGERS TP
ISBN: 978-1-58240-793-7
$12.99

VOL. 4: HEAD OF THE CLASS TP
ISBN: 978-1-58240-440-2
$14.95

VOL. 5: THE FACTS OF LIFE TP
ISBN: 978-1-58240-554-4
$14.99

VOL. 6: A DIFFERENT WORLD TP
ISBN: 978-1-58240-579-7
$14.99

VOL. 7: THREE'S COMPANY TP
ISBN: 978-1-58240-656-5
$14.99

VOL. 8: MY FAVORITE MARTIAN TP
ISBN: 978-1-58240-683-1
$14.99

VOL. 9: OUT OF THIS WORLD TP
ISBN: 978-1-58240-827-9
$14.99

VOL. 10: WHO'S THE BOSS TP
ISBN: 978-1-60706-013-0
$16.99

VOL. 11: HAPPY DAYS TP
ISBN: 978-1-60706-062-8
$16.99

VOL. 12: STILL STANDING TP
ISBN: 978-1-60706-166-3
$16.99

VOL. 13: GROWING PAINS TP
ISBN: 978-1-60706-251-6
$16.99

VOL. 14: THE VILTRUMITE WAR TP
ISBN: 978-1-60706-367-4
$19.99

ULTIMATE COLLECTION, VOL. 1 HC
ISBN 978-1-58240-500-1
$34.95

ULTIMATE COLLECTION, VOL. 2 HC
ISBN: 978-1-58240-594-0
$34.99

ULTIMATE COLLECTION, VOL. 3 HC
ISBN: 978-1-58240-763-0
$34.99

ULTIMATE COLLECTION, VOL. 4 HC
ISBN: 978-1-58240-989-4
$34.99

ULTIMATE COLLECTION, VOL. 5 HC
ISBN: 978-1-60706-116-8
$34.99

ULTIMATE COLLECTION, VOL. 6 HC
ISBN: 978-1-60706-360-5
$34.99

THE OFFICIAL HANDBOOK OF THE INVINCIBLE UNIVERSE TP
ISBN: 978-1-58240-831-6
$12.99

INVINCIBLE PRESENTS, VOL. 1: ATOM EVE & REX SPLODE TP
ISBN: 978-1-60706-255-4
$14.99

THE COMPLETE INVINCIBLE LIBRARY, VOL. 2 HC
ISBN: 978-1-60706-112-0
$125.00

THE WALKING DEAD

VOL. 1: DAYS GONE BYE TP
ISBN: 978-1-58240-672-5
$9.99

VOL. 2: MILES BEHIND US TP
ISBN: 978-1-58240-775-3
$14.99

VOL. 3: SAFETY BEHIND BARS TP
ISBN: 978-1-58240-805-7
$14.99

VOL. 4: THE HEART'S DESIRE TP
ISBN: 978-1-58240-530-8
$14.99

VOL. 5: THE BEST DEFENSE TP
ISBN: 978-1-58240-612-1
$14.99

VOL. 6: THIS SORROWFUL LIFE TP
ISBN: 978-1-58240-684-8
$14.99

VOL. 7: THE CALM BEFORE TP
ISBN: 978-1-58240-828-6
$14.99

VOL. 8: MADE TO SUFFER TP
ISBN: 978-1-58240-883-5
$14.99

VOL. 9: HERE WE REMAIN TP
ISBN: 978-1-60706-022-2
$14.99

VOL. 10: WHAT WE BECOME TP
ISBN: 978-1-60706-075-8
$14.99

VOL. 11: FEAR THE HUNTERS TP
ISBN: 978-1-60706-181-6
$14.99

VOL. 12: LIFE AMONG THEM TP
ISBN: 978-1-60706-254-7
$14.99

VOL. 13: TOO FAR GONE TP
ISBN: 978-1-60706-329-2
$14.99

VOL. 14: NO WAY OUT TP
ISBN: 978-1-60706-392-6
$14.99

BOOK ONE HC
ISBN: 978-1-58240-619-0
$34.99

BOOK TWO HC
ISBN: 978-1-58240-698-5
$34.99

BOOK THREE HC
ISBN: 978-1-58240-825-5
$34.99

BOOK FOUR HC
ISBN: 978-1-60706-000-0
$34.99

BOOK FIVE HC
ISBN: 978-1-60706-171-7
$34.99

BOOK SIX HC
ISBN: 978-1-60706-327-8
$34.99

DELUXE HARDCOVER, VOL. 2
ISBN: 978-1-60706-029-7
$100.00

DELUXE HARDCOVER, VOL. 3
ISBN: 978-1-60706-330-8
$100.00

THE WALKING DEAD: THE COVERS, VOL. 1 HC
ISBN: 978-1-60706-002-4
$24.99

REAPER

GRAPHIC NOVEL
ISBN: 978-1-58240-354-2
$6.95

SUPERPATRIOT

AMERICA'S FIGHTING FORCE
ISBN: 978-1-58240-355-1
$14.99

TECH JACKET

VOL. 1: THE BOY FROM EARTH TP
ISBN: 978-1-58240-771-5
$14.99

TALES OF THE REALM

HARDCOVER
ISBN: 978-1-58240-426-0
$34.95

TRADE PAPERBACK
ISBN: 978-1-58240-394-6
$14.95

TO FIND YOUR NEAREST COMIC BOOK STORE, CALL:
1-888-COMIC-BOOK